"I can take care of myself.

"So if you want more trouble than you can handle, just try treating me like a helpless woman again."

Alex grinned. "I haven't begun to treat you like a woman. When I do, I guarantee you won't complain."

Her eyes narrowed. "Don't hold your breath. It'll never happen."

"Wanna bet?"

She bit back a quick denial. He was a man who would know how to please a woman. The thought slipped into her consciousness, teasing her, horrifying her. Nothing in her life had prepared her for Alex Trent, but she would never turn her back on a dare. "Name the stakes."

"I'll wait till I win." He stuck out his hand, his grin wicked. "Deal?"

She was playing with fire. Even as the thought came to her, she was giving him her hand. "Deal."

Dear Reader,

This is a special month for Silhouette Intimate Moments, and those of you who have been with us from the beginning may know why. May 1988 marks our fifth anniversary, and what a lot has happened since May 1983, when we launched this new line with no idea how it would be received.

If we'd hoped for the best scenario we could imagine, we still might not have been able to come up with all the good things that have happened to these books and their authors. Silhouette Intimate Moments is selling better and better each month, thanks to you. And in return for your loyalty, we give you award-winning authors, books that consistently win the highest praise from romance reviewers, and a promise for the future: We will always be proud of everything we have done, but we will never rest on our laurels. In coming months, look for new miniseries from authors like Parris Afton Bonds and Emilie Richards, innovative books from longtime favorites like Kathleen Eagle and newcomers like Marilyn Pappano, and, of course, books that take no new chances at all but always live up to the standards we've set for this exciting line.

One last thing: Silhouette Intimate Moments has always been a line designed by the readers. It came into being because you told us you wanted stories that were not only longer but also bigger, larger than life, stories with mature characters, atypical plots and a strongly sensuous romance. Through the years you've never been shy about writing to me with compliments, complaints and suggestions. Now I want to renew our commitment to bringing you the books you want and to ask you, once again, to please keep writing to me. If we keep those lines of communication open, there's no telling how far we can go together.

Leslie J. Wainger
Senior Editor
Silhouette Intimate Moments

Linda Turner
The Echo of Thunder

Silhouette Intimate Moments

Published by Silhouette Books New York

America's Publisher of Contemporary Romance

SILHOUETTE BOOKS
300 East 42nd St., New York, N.Y. 10017

ISBN: 0-373-07238-4

First Silhouette Books printing May 1988

Printed in the U.S.A.

Books by Linda Turner

Silhouette Desire
A Glimpse of Heaven #220

Silhouette Special Edition
Shadows in the Night #350

Silhouette Intimate Moments
The Echo of Thunder #238

LINDA TURNER

is not only a writer but also a partner in a publishing company. She enjoys romance writing because it gives her a chance to travel extensively. She lives in Texas and hopes to sail someday from her home to Maine.

Prologue

The steel doors slammed shut with a chilling finality, but the man who followed the uniformed guard down the long corridor never even flinched. The sounds of prison were as familiar to him as the pounding of a judge's gavel, and the stale air of human confinement was a smell he had grown accustomed to. He'd long since ceased to wonder at the clinging cold or the ever-present feeling of being watched.

Alex Trent had never been disturbed by the watchfulness of others or by the unwritten rules of convention that often bound the rest of society. While most of his legal colleagues were clean-shaven and conservative, a dark, bushy mustache teased his upper lip, and his thick chestnut hair dared to brush the collar of his shirt. It was impossible not to notice his six feet two inches of hard, lean masculinity. And nature had fashioned his face on implacable lines, giving him rugged cheekbones, a blade of a nose and dimples that looked as if they'd been carved with a chisel. Despite his impeccably tailored navy suit and the sharp intelligence in his hazel eyes, he was a man with rough edges.

To the prostitutes, petty thieves and crooks who lived in the shadows of Phoenix's seamier side, Alex Trent was a straight shooter who spoke their language. He'd grown up walking the same streets they had, fighting just to survive. He knew what the taste of hunger and desperation could do to a man. Consequently he never sold anyone short, regardless of their ability to pay; and his reputation for pulling out all the stops for his clients was hard earned and well deserved. He played within the rules, but just barely.

He seldom lost.

The guard pushed open the door to the prison hospital and stopped at the entrance to a four-bed ward. "He's in here, Mr. Trent. The last bed by the window."

He'd expected to be shown to the visitor's gallery. Alex glanced sharply at the guard, his hazel eyes piercing. "What's wrong with him?"

"Cancer," the other man said flatly. "The doc told him to get his affairs in order. Guess that's why he wants to see you. Maybe he's going to make a will and leave all that money to the warden for taking such good care of him all these years."

Alex frowned at the guard's snide remark. Fifteen years earlier Harlan Perkins had been convicted of robbing three million dollars from a Phoenix bank and of killing two guards. Although he'd admitted his guilt regarding the theft, he'd claimed his partners, Joseph Maitland and Frank Graham, had set him up to take the rap for the murders. When pressed to reveal the whereabouts of the money, however, he'd refused. It had never been recovered, and the police had later learned that Frank and Joe had escaped to Brazil, presumably taking the money with them. After all these years of silence, it wasn't likely that Perkins would start talking now, even if he was dying.

So what did he want with a lawyer? Alex mused as he silently crossed the ward. He'd been wondering that ever since the old man had called yesterday and left a deliberately vague message with his secretary. Perkins had refused to say anything except that it was urgent that he see Alex as soon as possible.

The prisoner lying in the hospital bed hardly looked like a convicted killer. Harlan Perkins had the average, harmless sort of face that seldom draws attention to itself. He was wearing wire-rimmed glasses and gray pajamas, his gray hair was cropped short, his skin was pasty and pale from illness, and his large body seemed to have shrunk in upon itself. Alex thought he appeared listless, drained of energy, until he saw Harlan's ebony eyes. They were shrewd, bottomless, unsettling.

"You're Alex Trent." His words were sharp, gravelly, a statement rather than a question. "I wasn't sure you'd come."

"My curiosity got the best of me," Alex admitted, setting his briefcase on the portable table at the foot of the bed. His expression was rueful as he met the older man's steely gaze. "You've got quite a reputation."

A sardonic smile slid onto Harlan Perkins's face. "So do you. I heard you once took a jackass into a courtroom just to show the judge what one looked like."

Alex laughed, surprised, but his quick grin was unrepentant. "That was old Judge Hawkins. He almost got me for contempt on that one, but I won the case." Shoving his hands into the pockets of his slacks, he studied the other man with eyes that missed little. "I don't think you called me out here to talk about that, though, did you?"

"No." A sudden spasm of coughing racked the older man's large frame, and it was several moments before he could get his breath. Cursing his helplessness, he finally gasped fiercely, "I want you to clear my name. I won't die branded a murderer."

Offering no sympathy where he sensed none was wanted, Alex lifted his dark eyebrows mockingly. "I take it you have no objections to being labeled a bank robber?"

"I've never denied what I was. I was damned good at it."

"So good that you got caught," Alex remind him curtly. "You were found guilty of murder."

"I was framed!"

Alex snorted unbelievingly. "That story didn't wash fifteen years ago. Why should it now?"

"Because I can prove Joe Maitland killed those guards."

"How?"

"I know where the murder weapon is, and Joe's fingerprints are all over it."

Growing up in the slums of Phoenix, Alex had learned at an early age that there was no such thing as honor among thieves. A man who made a living breaking the law would say just about anything to save his own skin. Harlan Perkins was dying. How desperate was he to die a free man?

"Why didn't you come forward with this type of evidence during the trial?" Alex demanded suspiciously. "You could have cut years off your sentence."

"Because the gun's with the money. I didn't want to give it up." He leaned against the pillows propped at his back, and an almost feral gleam came into his black eyes. "You know what's so damn ironic? The cops think the money's in Brazil, and all these years its been right here in Arizona, practically within spitting distance. And I'm the only one who knows where it is."

Alex's eyes narrowed. The sixth sense that never failed him warned him that Harlan Perkins was making no idle boast. "What about your partners? Don't they know where it is?"

"No," he said smugly. "We knew the cops would be crawling all over the place after we hit that bank, and the only smart thing to do was hide the money and lay low for a while. I convinced Frank and Joe to let me hide it."

"Why you?"

"Because I knew this place up in the mountains where I used to go as a kid. It was perfect. I told the guys exactly where I'd bury it, and they agreed that I could be in and out before they could even find the place."

"If you think they're waiting on you to get out of prison to collect that three million, you've been in here too long," Alex retorted dryly.

"They waited, all right." Harlan laughed, the expression on his face hard as memories swept over him. "They had to. You see, I didn't trust Joe. Two weeks after the robbery we were all supposed to meet at an old house in Phoenix, go get the money and split it three ways. But I knew Joe would go back and get it if I hid it where we agreed. So I buried it somewhere else."

"And when you went to the rendezvous place—"

"The cops were waiting for me," Harlan said coldly. "Joe and Frank disappeared, making it look like they'd skipped the country, and I was left holding the bag. The bastards! But I had the last laugh. By the time they realized I'd tricked them, they couldn't get their hands on me or the money."

"And all these years you've been waiting for the day when you could get out and collect it all yourself," Alex guessed shrewdly. "The ultimate revenge."

"I've been counting the days for fifteen damn years," he growled. "For nothing! I'm up for parole in six months, but it might as well be six years. I'll never make it." His gaze locked with Alex's. "I'll die happy knowing Joe and Frank will never get their hands on that money. I want you to find it and get the murder conviction dropped. If there's still a reward, it's all yours. Are you interested?"

Interested? Sardonic laughter spilled into Alex's hazel eyes. Did the old man have any idea what he was asking? Fifteen years had passed since the robbery, fifteen long years in which evidence and money had lain hidden, waiting for someone to find them. The odds were that someone already had, and without the money and the gun, Harlan Perkins didn't have a chance in hell of beating his murder rap. A smart lawyer would have played the odds and told him to forget the past and accept the hand fate had dealt him. But Alex had never been one to play the odds.

"Why did you pick me to help you?" he asked suddenly. "You don't know me from Adam. For all you know, I could take the money, leave you here to die and be set for life."

Harlan's smile was hard, cold, dangerous. "Prison teaches you to be a damn good judge of character. I haven't lived with the scum of the earth for the last fifteen years without knowing who I can trust. You won't take the case unless you think you can clear me."

He was right, and they both knew it. Alex nodded. "You've got yourself a lawyer, Mr. Perkins. Where's the money?"

"About thirty-five miles from here, in the Superstition Mountains." Reaching for paper and a pencil on the bedside table, he drew a crude map. "That's virtually free money sitting up there in those mountains," he told Alex grimly as he handed him the map. "The bank's already collected on its insurance, the cops think it's in another country, and the case is closed. Anyone who finds it could keep it, no questions asked."

Alex looked at the paper in his hand and frowned. "This isn't a hell of a lot to go on."

"It is for someone who knows those mountains," the old man countered. "There's a guy by the name of Gus Dugan who knows every rock and canyon in that wilderness. He used to take the sheriff up on rescue operations, and he's got a reputation for being straight as an arrow. See if you can hire him as a guide. You're going to need somebody you can trust if you're going to get out of those mountains alive."

Chapter 1

The quiet was unnatural, ominous, heavy, broken only by the low, keening wail of the wind. A single gray cloud hovered on the western horizon, while dust swirled around the saguaro cacti that stood like sentinels in the empty, barren landscape of the desert. Jessica Rawlins stepped from her battered pickup, and her blue eyes narrowed as she looked at the cloud. She swept her straw cowboy hat from her head and wiped the sweat from her brow. A storm. She'd have known it was brewing even if she hadn't felt the restlessness building in her all day. She'd lived in the Arizona desert all her life, and she'd learned to read the weather before she'd learned to read a book. By the time that cloud reached her ranch, it would be a full-blown thunderstorm.

A fleeting thought that a little rain might break the sweltering heat was quickly dismissed. The water would hardly hit the dry, cracked earth before the sun would be out again, hotter than ever, the storm only a memory. Nothing lasted long in the desert, not horses, not people, and especially not water.

Frowning, Jessica plopped her hat back on her head and walked to the back of the truck to unload the stainless-steel canisters that filled the pickup bed. It looked as though there was enough water in those containers to float a small battleship, but Jessica knew she would be lucky if it lasted forty-eight hours. It didn't take long for three nine-year-old boys to go through water, especially in the summer. She only hoped Pete Smithers would find the problem with the well pump when he came out later that afternoon. She was tired of hauling water from the creek.

Sighing, she reached for another canister and transferred it to the barn. Years of working in the desert had taught her to pace herself to avoid heat exhaustion. She moved gracefully, her long legs covering the distance to the barn in four easy strides, the strain of carrying the heavy canisters visible only in the slight tightening of her jaw. The truck was half-empty when she finally stopped to take a break. The coolness of the barn felt like heaven, even though it was only ten degrees cooler than the ninety-eight outside.

She should have waited for the boys to help her, she silently admitted as she pulled her white shirt away from her body and fanned herself with her hat. The creek was one of their favorite summertime hangouts, and they'd be disappointed that she hadn't waited for them to get back from town. But the storm would probably arrive before they did, and she hadn't wanted to wait. She'd make it up to them by taking tomorrow afternoon off and spending it at the creek.

However, Charlie Smith, her ranch foreman, wouldn't be so easily appeased. He would have a fit when he learned she'd made the trip to the creek alone, but then Charlie had been scolding her about one thing or another since she'd been four years old. A slow grin spread across her heart-shaped face, and her blue eyes twinkled with fondness. Charlie didn't think it was seemly that a "lady" worked like a ranch hand when there were plenty of men around to do the heavy work. He'd say she was bullheaded, determined to have her own way come hell or high water, and that her grandfather should have taken her over his knee when he'd had the chance. She shouldn't have calluses on her hands or be so bone tired at night that she collapsed before it was even nine o'clock. And she sure as hell shouldn't ride and shoot like a man.

Charlie conveniently forgot that he was the one who had taught her to ride and shoot.

Jessica grinned. Poor Charlie. She supposed he and the other cowboys couldn't help it, but male chauvinism was alive and well on the Rabbit Creek Ranch and she'd been butting her head against it ever since she could remember. She'd tried pointing out to them that this was the 1980s and telling them they'd better wake up and smell the coffee before it was too late, but it was useless. When they looked at her, they didn't see the woman she'd become but rather the little girl they remembered riding hell-bent for leather on her pony, her black pigtails flying out behind her. Over the years they'd all come to an unspoken agreement—they'd still protect her at every turn, and she'd pretend she didn't notice. Everyone was happy, she thought with a chuckle as she stepped into the sun again to resume her work.

Later she couldn't say what had warned her she was no longer alone. Maybe it was the whisper of a footstep on the gravel path that led from the house, or perhaps the eerie, unexpected touch of someone staring at her. But suddenly the fine hairs at the nape of her neck were tingling in alarm. She whirled, and her breath caught at the sight of the stranger standing watching her at the corner of the barn.

Tension crackled in the air like raw electricity, and for what seemed like an eternity the only sound she heard was her heartbeat thundering in her ears. Where had he come from? Jessica wondered frantically. He'd materialized out of nowhere, a dark, looming figure with a face as hard and rough as the desert terrain. In spite of the chinos and the white safari shirt he wore, there was something a little bit uncivilized about him. An image of the unsavory characters that sometimes wandered down onto the ranch from the nearby mountains suddenly flashed before her eyes, and without stopping to think, Jessica snatched up the rifle in the truck's cab and pointed it right at the stranger's heart.

The soft click of the hammer being pulled back was like an explosion. Alex froze, anger flickering in the depths of his hazel eyes as he surveyed the woman before him. He didn't like guns, and he sure as hell didn't like them pointed at him without reason. Especially by a woman.

"Lady," he drawled mockingly, "I sure hope you know how to use that thing, because I'd hate for it to go off by accident."

"If it goes off, it'll be no accident," she retorted coldly. She steadied her grip on the rifle, and a trace of fear shadowed her icy blue eyes. Inside, she was shaking like a leaf, but she'd have died before she let this man know it. Some men thrived on fear. "I can shoot you right between the eyes before you even blink."

Alex didn't doubt for a minute that she was deadly serious. She handled the rifle with a sureness that came only from long practice, and there was something in her expression that told him she wasn't the type to make idle threats. A tough lady, he decided. And incredibly pretty in spite of the jeans, work shirt and cowboy hat that halfheartedly disguised a cloud of midnight-black hair. With her high cheekbones, wide-set blue eyes and soft, sensuous mouth, she could have turned heads on a crowded city street. In the desolation of the desert, she was breathtaking.

"Bloodthirsty, aren't you? It really isn't necessary, you know. I don't know what you think I did, but I'm innocent."

Jessica gave an unladylike snort. Innocent? She doubted he'd ever been innocent. He had the hard, cynical looks of a man who had seen just about everything. And if he thought that smile of his would relax her guard, he was in for a rude awakening. "Who are you and what do you want?"

"Alex Trent." He started to reach for his identification, then cursed in frustration when she stiffened warningly. His mouth thinned in irritation. "Damn it, I was just reaching for my wallet. I'm a lawyer. From Phoenix. I'm looking for Gus Dugan."

A second glance at his clothes showed Jessica they were far too expensive to belong to a mountain derelict. Making no apologies for pulling a gun on him, she lowered the rifle until it was pointed at the ground. "Gus Dugan was my grandfather. Did you have business with him?"

Alex shot her a sharp look. "Was?"

"He died six months ago."

"I'm sorry," he said sincerely. "I'd heard he knew the Superstition Mountains better than just about anyone, and I was hoping to hire him as a guide."

Another tourist chasing rainbows, Jessica thought in disgust. Somehow she hadn't really expected that of this man. He didn't look like the type that believed in pipe dreams.

Her gaze automatically lifted to the mountains that sat, dark and brooding, right at the edge of her ranch.

She tried to view them dispassionately. The Superstitions. They dominated the desert landscape for miles around, their sheer, slick cliffs impregnable but for the twisting maze of deadly crevices and canyons at their base. According to legend, the elusive Lost Dutchman Mine lay hidden somewhere within those rocky spires. It had lured countless prospectors to their deaths with the promise of a king's ransom in lost gold.

Geologists claimed the mine didn't even exist, but that hadn't stopped her grandfather from looking for it. The day he'd died, he'd been planning another trip into the Superstitions.

Turning away abruptly, Jessica laid the rifle across the pickup's front seat. "There are several tour operations in town that will take you into the mountains for a fair price, Mr. Trent. Try one of them." Without another word, she disappeared into the barn.

Alex scowled. A tour operation was the last thing he wanted. It was too organized, too public, and the less people who knew about his trip into the mountains the better. He needed someone he could trust, someone who wouldn't be reporting back to an office and giving out his location to anyone who cared to listen.

Impatiently pushing his hair back from his sweaty brow, he strode into the barn. Cool shadows immediately enveloped him, and it was several seconds before his eyes adjusted to the change in light. When they did, he saw Gus Dugan's granddaughter shutting the wide double doors at the other end of the building.

He started forward to help her, only to stop, the look in her eyes clearly telling him she didn't want or need his assistance. He growled, "Look, lady, if you'll just give me a few minutes of your time, I'll be out of your hair and you can get back to your work."

Jessica slammed the doors. "The name isn't 'Lady,' " she said softly, her blue eyes flashing as she passed him to close the doors at the other end. "It's Jessica Rawlins. *Mrs*. Rawlins. And if you're going to get out of here before that storm hits, you'd better talk fast."

For the first time, Alex noticed the whine of the wind beating at the old barn. In the distance, the echo of thunder rumbled in the mountains. She was right; he didn't have much time. Once the rain started, the dirt road back to the highway would quickly turn into a quagmire.

"I'm not really interested in going to a tour operation," he explained, following her over to the partially open door where she watched the storm approach. "I was hoping you might know of another rancher around here that might know the mountains as well as your grandfather did. I need to get up there as quickly as possible."

"In this heat?" she asked mockingly, dragging her gaze away from the horizon to look at the man beside her. "Even if I could recommend someone, which I can't, you wouldn't find any rancher crazy enough to go up in those mountains this time of year.

Oh, sure, the guides will take you up. They'll do just about anything for money, but nobody else will. Wait till winter."

He couldn't wait, damn it! He'd had a talk with Harlan's doctor before he'd left the prison, and the news hadn't been encouraging. He had two months at the most.

"I can't wait," Alex said flatly. "What about your husband? Maybe he could—"

Jessica cut him off curtly. "I'm a widow. There's no one here who can help you."

"What about you?" he demanded, eyeing her appraisingly. "Did you ever go up in the mountains with your grandfather?"

Jessica knew exactly where his questions were leading. As a child she'd been as fascinated by the mountains as her grandfather, and she'd spent a lot of hours up there exploring with him. Yes, she knew those mountains—every cliff and canyon, every rock. She also knew just how deadly they could be. She'd watched her husband die there.

"Yes, I know the mountains," she finally replied, moving away from him. "But I won't take you."

Stepping into her path, Alex cut her off, his gaze boring into hers in the barn's gloomy light. "I'll make it worth your while," he promised. "Double the usual fee."

"I'm not interested in your money, Mr. Trent. Find yourself someone else. I don't go up in the mountains anymore."

"Why?"

The question was quick, sharp. Jessica's expressive face became closed. "That's none of your business," she said coldly.

No, it wasn't, Alex admitted, irritation darkening his brow. But he wasn't taking no for an answer, damn it! Time was running out, and he couldn't waste it scouring the countryside for someone who both knew the mountains as well as Gus Dugan and was trustworthy. Instinct already told him he'd found that person in Jessica Rawlins. He hadn't even considered hiring a woman, but he could tell that this was no ordinary woman. She might be beautiful, but she was also stubborn, independent and a gun-toting Annie Oakley who could take care of herself. She was just what he needed.

He reached into his back pocket for his wallet and the map he had hidden there. "I wasn't going to show you this just yet, but maybe it will help change your mind. I've got a map."

How many times had she heard that phrase? Jessica wondered sardonically. People had come from all over the world to search for the Lost Dutchman, and every one of them had had a map.

"I hope you didn't pay too much for it," she said mockingly. "They're a dime a dozen at the local flea market."

Exasperated, Alex shoved his wallet back into his pocket, his eyes glittering as they locked with hers. The lady had a sassy tongue. "I'll give you five percent of what I find up there, Mrs. Rawlins. Think about it before you say anything," he cautioned. "If you turn me down, you'll be giving up a lot of money." One hundred and fifty thousands dollars, he silently added.

He was serious. He really expected to find the lost mine, even though people had been looking for it for over a century! Her lips twitched. "Five percent of nothing is still nothing," she said gently, as if he were dim-witted. "Sorry, but I'm not interested."

His mouth thinned at her tone. "You don't know what you're doing, Mrs. Rawlins," he growled. "You're making a terrible mistake."

The mistake would have been accepting his offer. She'd seen enough of Alex Trent to know she didn't want to have anything to do with him. He was too sure of himself, too used to getting his own way. The women in his life might let him get away with murder, but Jessica had been fighting for her independence all her life and she'd learned a long time ago how to hold her own with domineering males.

Tilting her head to one side, she pushed back her cowboy hat and studied him curiously. "Hasn't anyone ever told you no before?"

"Oh, I've heard the word," he said silkily. "I've just never let it stop me. What will it take to get you to change your mind?"

Jessica's gaze moved past his shoulder to the open doorway of the barn. There in the distance, shrouded in rain, the mountains sat dark and mysterious, deadly. When she looked at Alex again, her expression was empty. "Nothing you have to offer, Mr. Trent. Sorry."

Like hell she was sorry! He marched over to the open door, pausing only long enough to glare at her in frustration. "If you change your mind," he said curtly, "I'm staying at the Desert Inn." Turning, he strode angrily out into the gathering storm.

Chapter 2

The storm was only a memory two hours later. Jessica collapsed on the old wicker settee on the back porch and groaned out of sheer exhaustion as her hat slid down over her eyes. Every bone in her body ached, and there was so much dirt and grime on her skin that it felt like sandpaper. She'd have killed for a long soak in the tub, but she knew from experience that it would be several days before they had the luxury of running water. Pete Smithers had finally arrived to look at the pump, but it would probably take him a while to locate the out-of-date parts for the ancient equipment. Until then, she thought with a grimace, she'd have to make do with another sponge bath.

A door slammed. Jessica glanced up in time to see Pete place his tools in his truck and come toward her in a loping gate that was peculiarly his own. Pete was a thin, wiry man who had more lines etched in his brow than he had hairs on his balding head, and he had the demeanor of a perpetual worrier. Jessica had learned long ago that things were seldom as grim as Pete painted them.

She gave him a fond grin as he came onto the porch. "That was fast. The pump's on its last legs, isn't it? I figured as much. It would have given out years ago if you hadn't babied it the way you have."

Pete eased down into the old wicker rocker that flanked the settee and mopped his sweaty brow with his handkerchief. The pale blue eyes behind the lenses of his thick glasses were troubled. "Jessie, I hate to tell you this, but the news isn't good."

She'd expected no less. Her lips twitched. "I know. We need a new pump. You've been telling me that for years, but the boys always needed one thing or another and the pump had to wait. God knows where I'm going to get the money this time." She sighed. "How much will a new one cost?"

Somehow, Pete's lined face became even grimmer. "It's not the pump, Jessie," he said gently. "It's the well itself. It's just about dry."

She blinked, convinced she hadn't heard correctly. "What do you mean it's dry? Three days ago it was fine."

He shook his head. "That well hasn't had good pressure for over a year. I can't believe it's lasted this long."

"But it can't be dry!" Her eyes flew to the small outbuilding that housed the pump, a sick feeling of dread rolling into her stomach. "How can you be sure? If the pump's acting up—"

"The pump's working fine, but it can't pull up water if there's none there." He leaned back, hating what he had to say but knowing he had no other choice. "You're going to have to put in another well."

She wanted to laugh at the utter simplicity of his words but was afraid she would cry instead. She'd been worried about where she would come up with the money for a pump. And now he was saying she needed a new well! "How much is this going to cost?" she asked hoarsely.

"Five if you're lucky, up to eight if you're not. It just depends on how deep we've got to drill."

She paled. Lucky? He was talking five to eight *thousand* dollars! It might as well have been five to eight million. It had been years since the ranch had had that kind of money.

To an outsider it might look as if she were sitting pretty, but looks were deceptive. The adobe ranch house had foot-thick walls, Mexican tile floors and beamed cedar ceilings. Ceiling fans and wide paned windows contributed to a feeling of rich, cool spaciousness, but the antique furniture and Indian rugs scattered about the house were remnants of a more profitable time in the ranch's history. The property was mortgaged to the hilt, and the insurance money she'd received after her husband's death had been used up years before. The last time she'd gone to the bank for a loan, the loan officer had warned her she'd have to pay something off before the bank could extend her any more credit. But the cattle industry was still in a slump, and there was no relief in sight.

Now they were out of water. Dear God, where was she going to get the money for a new well?

Alex Trent.

His name popped into her head unbidden, unwanted, the image of his dark, good-looking face springing to mind all too easily. No! she told herself furiously. She'd already given him her answer. She wasn't going into those mountains with him or anyone else. She wouldn't even consider it. She had to find another way to raise the money!

Frowning at the desperation of her thoughts, she forced herself to remain calm. She couldn't afford the luxury of panic. Not now, not ever. Too many people depended on her.

"Jessie, I can cut you a little slack if you need some time to come up with the money," Pete offered hesitantly. He'd known her since she was a little girl, and he knew her pride. For years, pride and sheer guts had been all she'd had to keep the ranch going. "You can't keep hauling water from the creek for you and those boys of yours. Not in this heat. Everybody's having a rough time right now—"

She was shaking her head before the words were even out of his mouth. Pete was an old friend of her grandfather's, and she couldn't—wouldn't—take advantage of his friendship. "Now, Pete, you know I couldn't do that, but I appreciate the offer."

"Well, you can't stay out here without water, that's for sure," he grumbled, not surprised by her refusal. She never had been one to accept help easily. "What you gonna do?"

"I don't know," she said as she got to her feet and stared out at the endless acres of her ranch. "I'll think of something. I always do."

But that evening, as she sat down to supper, she was still drawing a frustrating blank. She'd racked her brain for a possible source of cash, and the only answer she'd come up with was Alex Trent. Damn the man, why did he keep haunting her? He was arrogant and cynical, and she had no intention of going anywhere with him, least of all into the Superstitions.

There had to be another way.

Name one, a voice in her head taunted. Where else can you get the type of money he's offering? Take it and run.

In growing disgust, she had to admit she was tempted. Double the usual fee plus five percent of whatever he found was nothing to sneeze at. What if he really found something? She might have turned down a fortune.

Wincing, she suddenly realized where her thoughts had wandered. She was beginning to sound like her grandfather! Every time he'd gone into the mountains he'd promised to bring her a gold nugget from the Lost Dutchman. And every time he'd come home he'd been empty-handed.

"Are you going to eat those peas or push them around your plate all night?" Mary Lou Hopkins asked dryly.

Jessica glanced up at the large, rawboned woman who sat next to her. On the downhill side of sixty and not the least bit disturbed by it, Mary Lou had come to the ranch over fifteen years ago because Gus Dugan had insisted Jessica needed a woman's influence. Jessica had always suspected he'd hired the older woman because he couldn't abide Jessica's cooking.

Shrugging ruefully, Jessica dropped her fork on her plate and gave up all pretense of eating. "Sorry, Mary Lou. I seem to have lost my appetite."

"Starving yourself isn't going to solve anything," the older woman muttered irritably.

"How can I eat when all I can think about is five thousand dollars? Where am I going to come up with that kind of money?"

"You could sell off that forty acres Able Dawkins has been hounding you for," Charlie said suddenly from the other end of the table, his thick salt-and-pepper eyebrows knitted over his nose, his green eyes intense in his craggy face. Jessica had told him about the well as soon he'd returned from town with Mary Lou and the boys, and he'd been mulling over the problem ever since. "He'd be tickled pink to take it off your hands."

"He's been after that land for as long as I've been here," Mary Lou said, starting to whisk the dirty dishes from the table. Laughter deepened the already deep lines in her plain face. "Every fall he pestered Gus to let him have that land, and every fall Gus told him no." She chuckled. "He'd storm out of here cussin' a blue streak."

Charlie snorted disdainfully. "Dawkins is an old miser. Even if you did decide to sell him that land, he'd want you to practically give it to him, he's so tight." He glanced at the three boys sitting in a row on the other side of the table and winked slyly. "Why, he passed me this afternoon outside the feed store, and I swear he squeaks when he walks."

Three identical pairs of mischievous blue eyes looked expectantly at the old man sitting across the kitchen table. Charlie always kept the triplets entertained at mealtimes.

"I didn't hear anything, Charlie," Matthew said with a frown.

"Me, neither," Mark echoed, his round, freckled face an exact copy of his two brothers'. "And I was standing right next to him."

"I did," John piped up, an impish grin tugging at the corners of his mouth. "Squeak, squeak. Just like the Tin Man in *The Wizard of Oz*."

"John," Jessica said reprovingly, her lips twitching traitorously as she tried to hold back a smile. Discipline was such a problem when they always made her want to laugh. Her sons were nine going on forty, and she never knew what they were going to do or say next. "I'm sure Mr. Dawkins doesn't squeak."

The youngest by fifteen minutes, John considered her argument and finally nodded his dark head. "I think he squished instead. He'd just stepped into a puddle with his new boots, and boy, was he mad!"

The other two boys giggled, and Jessica, giving up the struggle to appear stern, joined in. They could see right through her, anyway. She lifted dancing eyes to Charlie. "One of these days they're going to embarrass the devil out of you for saying things like that, and I hope I'm there to see it."

"Aw, Jessie, I'm just having a little fun. Me and the boys understand each other."

"That's what I'm afraid of," she muttered, still smiling. Her gaze dropped to the table, where she absently traced a circle of moisture left by her iced-tea glass. When she looked up again, the laughter was gone and there was a determined set to her jaw that was all too familiar to the group seated around the table. "I'm not going to sell to Dawkins. Grandpa always said we were land-rich and money-poor and—"

"If you start selling off the land when you get in a bind, it won't be long before you'll be nothing but poor," Mary Lou finished for her. "So what are you going to do?"

Jessica hesitated, her gaze going to her sons. "You guys finished?" At their nod, she said, "Why don't you go watch the movies you rented in town?" She didn't have to make the suggestion twice. With a whoop of glee, they jumped up and headed for the living room.

Jessica watched them go before she turned back to the two old friends who had ceased to be employees years before. "We had another visitor this afternoon besides Pete. A lawyer from Phoenix looking for someone to take him up into the mountains. I'm going to do it."

Charlie looked at her as if she'd lost her mind. "Damn it, girl, you can't be serious!" he exclaimed. "You hate those mountains!"

She nodded. Yes, she hated them, and no one knew that better than Charlie and Mary Lou. They'd been there when she'd come down out of the mountains all those years before, a widow at nineteen. Six months later she'd given birth to the boys. "We need that new well, Charlie. If I can earn some money as a guide, I'd be a fool not to take it."

"Maybe you could try the bank again," Mary Lou suggested, with concern. "Surely if you explained the situation to them they'd give the loan."

"I called Mark Zimmerman at the bank after Pete left," she said. "He was sorry, but he couldn't help me."

Charlie swore furiously. "Damn it, I don't like it! You've got no business traipsing around those mountains with some fancy-pants lawyer who probably doesn't know one end of a horse from another. You haven't been up there in a long time—"

"The mountains haven't changed," Jessica cut in stiffly. As a teenager, she'd balked at the overprotectiveness he and the other ranch hands had shown her. They'd worried about her long after her grandfather had realized she was capable of taking care of herself. But that had been years before. Time and maturity had taught her patience, though it wasn't a lesson she always remembered. "I'm not stupid enough to underestimate the mountains, Charlie. I'll never make that mistake again."

He was far from satisfied, but he knew from the glint in her eye that there was no changing her mind. Scowling, he pushed back his chair and got to his feet. Lean and weathered as an old fence post, he glared at her in frustration. "You always were bullheaded. I can see there's no talking any sense to you tonight. Maybe tomorrow you'll be more reasonable."

He stomped out without a backward glance, letting the screen door slam behind him. A tense silence echoed in his wake. Jessica sighed and resisted the urge to call him back. "I knew he would react that way."

Mary Lou, never one to beat about the bush, said, "If Charlie had his way, you'd still be in pigtails. Give him some time to cool off. He'll come around."

"I wish I could," Jessica said wistfully. "But time is one thing I haven't got." Pushing away from the table, she stood abruptly. "I've got to get into town before that lawyer finds himself another guide. If he hasn't already."

The ride into town was over all too soon. For several long moments after she pulled into the parking lot of the Desert Inn, Jessica sat in the darkness staring blindly at the adobe building. Irritation feathered across her brow. Damn Alex Trent! He'd been so sure that he had only to throw his money around to get what he wanted. And now here she was running after him, proving him right. It was positively galling.

But what choice did she have? She needed money, and he had it. Her shoulders stiff with pride, she reluctantly stepped from the truck.

The Desert Inn was the closest thing Apache Junction had to a five-star hotel. As Jessica stepped into the inn's quietly elegant lobby, she suddenly wished she'd worn something other than jeans and a yellow peasant blouse. But she wasn't there to impress Alex Trent, she reminded herself.

The desk clerk gave her his room number without consulting the register, then promptly informed Jessica he wasn't there. He'd gone into the lounge about fifteen minutes before, and she hadn't seen him come out. Stifling the urge to return to the ranch before she made a horrible mistake, Jessica smiled her thanks and stepped into the open doorway of the lounge at the far end of the lobby.

The soft glow of candles pushed at the shadows darkening the bar's intimate corners, and laughter and murmured conversations drifted on fingers of cigarette smoke that spiraled toward the ceiling. It was a Friday night and the lounge was fairly full, with most of the tables occupied. A few businessmen nursed their drinks in quiet solitude at one end of the long mahogany bar. At the other, Alex Trent grinned at a bleached blonde in a skintight halter dress who was all but rubbing up against him to get his attention.

Jessica stiffened, annoyance stirring in her. Why was she surprised? From the moment she'd laid eyes on Alex Trent, she'd known there was an air of danger about him that most women would find hard to resist. For reasons Jessica refused to examine too closely, that irritated the hell out of her.

"It's a wonder he goes anywhere without a bodyguard," she muttered irritably, stepping purposefully into the bar. The sooner she got this over with, the better.

The blonde was the first to notice Jessica. Her baby-blue eyes narrowed dangerously as she laid a possessive hand on Alex's thigh and leaned over to whisper in his ear. When he laughed mockingly, the look she shot Jessica dared her to intrude.

Never one to ignore a dare, Jessica stepped closer. "Mr. Trent," she said stiffly, "I hate to interrupt, but I need to talk to you for a minute."

Alex swiveled around on his bar stool. The laughter that had transformed his face didn't falter at the sight of her. But something in his eyes turned hard. "Well, well, if it isn't Mrs. Rawlins," he drawled. "I almost didn't recognize you without your rifle."

Jessica grimaced. "Can we talk?"

When he'd wanted to talk to her at her ranch, she'd dismissed him as if he had been a drifter in search of a handout. It would serve her right if he gave her a little of her own medicine. "Talk away," he taunted in a bored tone, reaching for his drink. "It's a free country."

Jessica almost kicked him. She would have liked nothing better than to turn on her heel and walk out, but she needed him. "I've been thinking over your offer," she admitted coolly. "I've changed my mind. If you haven't found someone else, I'm available."

"He's already found someone for the night," the blonde protested angrily. "Go find your own man. This one's taken."

"Now, now, girls..." Alex laughed, amusement dancing in his eyes as he watched the heat climb in Jessica's cheeks. "Don't fight." When she sent him a withering glance, his grin broadened. "Have a drink," he told the blonde as he got to his feet. "The lady and I have something to discuss." Before either woman could protest, he took Jessica's elbow and guided her to one of the lounge's dark, intimate corners.

They were already at a small, candlelit table before Jessica thought to pull her arm from his hold. When he pulled out a chair next to his, she defiantly ignored it and took a seat on the opposite side of the table. Instinct warned her that he was a man who took charge without asking and that she'd regret it if she didn't take a stand from the very beginning. Folding her hands, she met his gaze head-on. "Now, Mr. Trent, about your offer..."

His eyes glinting dangerously, Alex took the seat she'd ignored. The irritation that had been simmering in him ever since he'd left her ranch was quickly coming to a boil. He'd spent the better part of the afternoon checking out the local tour operations, and it had been nothing but a damn waste of time. Life had taught him not to trust lightly, and the only person he felt he could put any faith in was Jessica Rawlins. He didn't know what it was about her that reassured him—maybe the fact that she'd tossed his money back in his face as if he'd insulted her—but his instinct told him he could trust her with his life. He wouldn't accept anything less from a guide he'd hire to take him into the mountains. But her manners left a lot to be desired.

He eyed the challenging lift of her chin and bit back a sudden grin. The lady needed to be brought down a notch or two, and he was just the person to do it.

He leaned back in his chair. "Sorry," he said without the least sign of remorse. "You're too late."

She paled. "You mean you've found someone else?"

"No, I mean the offer I made you this afternoon has expired. If you want to be my guide, you'll have to renegotiate."

Anger flickered in her eyes. "I wouldn't have thought you were the type of man to go back on your word, Mr. Trent."

He grinned. He had every intention of paying her the full amount, but he couldn't resist teaching her a badly needed lesson. "The name's Alex, and I'm not going back on my word. You rejected my earlier offer, so now I'm making a counter offer. Two-fifty a day, and I won't go a penny higher."

"But that's ridiculous. That's fifty dollars less than what you offered this afternoon!"

"Now it's two hundred."

"Two hundred! But you just said two-fifty—"

"I told you I wouldn't go any higher. It can only go down. One fifty."

Outraged, she sputtered, "But—"

"One hundred," he teased. She was furious. And gorgeous. His grin broadened. "If you want to make anything out of this deal, you'd better snap it up before you find yourself taking me up into the mountains for free."

"Of all the low-down, despicable—" She glared at him in frustration, a string of colorful curses she'd picked up from Charlie trembling on her tongue. Then suddenly, she saw the mischief glittering in his eyes. She let out her breath in a huff, the angry words dying unspoken in her throat.

He was joking.

Torn between indignation and amusement, Jessica didn't know whether she wanted to kick him or kiss him in relief. Her eyes searched his dancing ones before dropping to the wicked laughter curving the sensuous mouth beneath the bushy mustache. Somewhere deep inside her a long-forgotten awareness stirred, startling her.

Good Lord, what was she doing? she wondered. The man had a certain roguish charm, but she'd grown up on a ranch full of cowboys and she'd learned a long time ago how to handle charm.

Forcing herself to relax, she gave him an easy smile. "Next time I won't be so gullible, Mr. Trent."

He flashed his dimples outrageously. "Alex," he reminded her. "You might as well use it, because I don't intend to go up into those mountains calling you Mrs. Rawlins. Now, Jessica, about your fee—"

"Three hundred a day," she answered promptly, all business. At his amused look, she said defensively, "You said double the usual fee, and I'm holding you to it. That'll include horses, all equipment, and food, of course."

"Of course," he said dryly. "I'll need two of your ranch hands. Preferably two you can trust."

"I can trust *all* my hands. What do you need them for?"

"To dig, so the bigger and stronger they are the better."

"Then you'll want Slim Farrell. He's built like a linebacker and as strong as an ox. He's worked for me for over ten years now, and I've never known him to get into any kind of trouble. You can trust him."

He nodded. "Sounds like he'll do. Who else?"

"Charlie Smith. He's my ranch foreman and as straight as they come. He's not big like Slim, but he's tough. And the two of them together are going to cost you another hundred a day," she warned. "They weren't part of the original deal."

Alex saw the stubborn set of her jaw and he laughed suddenly. "Your hands aren't the only ones who are tough. You drive a hard bargain, but you've got yourself a deal." He extended his hand across the table, the candlelight sculpting his face in sensuous shadows, his hazel eyes snaring hers. "Shall we shake on it?"

A simple handshake. Jessica gave him her hand, her palm sliding along his as his fingers closed over hers. Suddenly it wasn't simple at all. Heat seemed to jump from his hands to hers, warming her, scattering her pulse. Caught in his watchful gaze, she needed every ounce of her control to keep from jerking free of his touch. Instead she calmly pulled her hand from his and gave him a cool smile. But inside she was shaking.

"Now that that's settled—" she said in an amazingly steady voice, "—I need to see the map and check out our destination so I'll know how much food to take. How long are you planning on staying up there?"

Alex stared at her for a long, tense moment, frowning as he searched the delicate lines of her face. Her hand, a fascinating mixture of calluses, strength and delicacy, was smaller than he'd expected. She was, he mused, a woman well used to hard work. Why, then, did he have this sudden urge to wrap her in silk? She'd be beautiful in silk.

He swore silently. He'd been working too hard, he decided. Determinedly, he reached for his wallet after making sure their table was well-secluded, away from any interested eyes. Pulling out the map, he handed it to her. "I'll stay as long as it takes to find what I'm looking for," he said quietly. "It could be just a few days or weeks. I won't know until I get up there.''

He really expected to find something. Amazed by his confidence, Jessica carefully unfolded the crudely drawn map and held it close to the candle to study it. Uneasiness stirred in her when she saw where he wanted to go. When she looked up at him again, her blue eyes were troubled. "I don't know how much you know about the Superstitions, but the Apaches believe the mountains are the home of their thunder god." She tapped a section of the map with the tip of her finger. "This area right here is their most sacred ground, and you want to dig right in the middle of it. They don't take kindly to trespassers.''

She was so serious that Alex couldn't help but laugh. "You don't really believe in all that nonsense, do you? Come on, this is the twentieth century, not the Dark Ages.''

"It doesn't matter whether I believe it or not." She shrugged and returned the map to him. "The Indians do. They've caused trouble before. They might do it again.''

"I doubt it, but I'll take my chances," he said, casually dismissing her warning. "When can we leave?''

Jessica bit her lips as she thought about everything that had to be done. The minute she got back to the ranch, she'd call Pete and tell him he could start drilling the new well as soon as possible. Then there were the boys to think of. She'd never been away from them for any length of time. "I'll have to get supplies and make arrangements for some work to be done at the ranch. I can't possibly be ready before the day after tomorrow.''

That would mean another day lost, but it would have to do. He nodded. "I'll be ready."

"Then I guess I'll see you out at the ranch Sunday morning," she said, standing. "We'll leave at dawn and get as far as we can before the heat hits."

Alex studied her, puzzled. "What happened?" he asked before she could leave. "This afternoon you seemed pretty determined not to go anywhere near those mountains. I'm not fool enough to think it was my boyish charm that changed your mind."

She hesitated, her gaze running over his lean, hard frame before coming back to his face. He had charm, all right, more than any one man deserved, but she wasn't about to admit that, now or ever. Arching a brow in amusement, she told him the truth without knowing it was the last thing in the world he really wanted to hear. "It's nice to know I won't be going into the mountains with a fool, Alex. Only one thing could get me up there right now, and that's money. You made me an offer I couldn't refuse."

Chapter 3

The sun beat down fiercely on the dusty, barren mountains, discouraging all signs of life but the stubborn prickly pear, the saguaro cactus and the catclaw that clung to the jagged cliffs and deep ravines. Although it was barely ten o'clock in the morning, the temperature was in the low nineties. Before the day was over it would reach well into the hundreds, and the heat, which was now merely stifling, would become unbearable. The sun was already starting to bleach the cloudless sky white.

The trail was a well-marked series of switchbacks that Jessica knew like the back of her hand. The path zigzagged up into the connecting canyons that offered the only access to the mountains. It was rough and steep, strewn with boulders and loose gravel that made any kind of speed impossible. The four riders and three pack mules loaded down with camping gear and supplies had been climbing steadily since they'd left the ranch at dawn. It seemed like they'd hardly covered any distance at all. Their destination was still several days away.

Alex Trent was already seething at the slow pace. From behind her, Jessica could feel him glaring at her back. They hadn't even left the ranch when he'd taken one look at the three pack mules and asked sarcastically if she'd remembered to bring the kitchen sink.

Her sapphire eyes flashed at the memory. They'd had words, of course, and instinct warned her they were just the first of many. The man was impossible! She'd known he was going to be trouble the minute she'd seen him, and if she'd had any sense she'd have charged him another hundred dollars a day for the agitation she knew he'd cause. If he was in such an all-fired rush to start his damn prospecting, he should have hired himself a helicopter instead of a guide. She knew better than to hurry in the Superstitions.

The mountains. They hadn't changed in all these years. Memories assaulted her at every turn. For one anguished moment, she closed her eyes against the sight of them, surrounding her, threatening her. But she couldn't close her mind to the haunting stillness that was such a tangible part of the Superstitions. The absence of sound rang in her ears like a scream.

How could she have thought she could come back into the Superstitions and not feel the past, the pain?

Her horse snorted suddenly and increased its pace, bringing Jessica's attention back to the path with a start. Up ahead, the trail narrowed and squeezed between two familiar enormous boulders. She sighed in relief. The first rest stop. Anyone who knew the mountains was familiar with the spring concealed in the rugged terrain on the other side of those rocks. She and her grandfather had never come into the mountains without stopping there.

Alex wouldn't like it, but this time she would welcome his impatience. It would take her mind off her surroundings. Cautiously steering her sorrel through the big rocks, she pulled up on the other side and turned to watch the three men as they followed her.

Alex eased his big bay through the rocks with a skill that surprised Jessica. It also irritated her, she admitted honestly. She'd expected him to be a fish out of water on a horse. The man was a lawyer, for God's sake, who spent his days in the air-conditioned courtrooms of Phoenix. He should already have been sore from the ride and swearing at the heat. Instead he looked as if he'd been born on a horse. His jeans and long-sleeved Western shirt were well worn, and his battered straw cowboy hat reminded her of one her grandfather had refused to part with because it was so comfortable. She glanced at Alex's feet, and her annoyance warred with a grudging respect. He'd even had the sense to wear leather tennis shoes, which would be much safer on the rocks than boots.

"Something wrong?" Alex drawled.

Her gaze snapped back to him, heat climbing into her cheeks as she realized he'd caught her studying him. "I was just wondering where you'd learned to ride," she said stiffly.

"I spent my summer vacations working on a ranch when I was in college. Why? Is there a problem?"

The problem was that he looked too darn good, but she'd have died rather than admit that. "No," she said abruptly. "I'm just glad you know what you're doing. These mountains aren't the place to learn how to ride."

She turned to see Slim Farrell come through the rocks. A large bear of a man with a quiet manner, he had plain, homely features and short brown hair that he'd worn in a crew cut since long before that style had again become fashionable. He had a reputation for avoiding trouble like the plague, and in all the years she'd known him, she'd never once heard him raise his voice in anger.

Charlie brought up the rear, grumbling about the heat, the dust and the mountains in general. The armpit of the earth, he called them; and the only time he went into them was to rescue stray cattle that were too dumb to know they were wandering into a death trap. He'd made no secret that he didn't like what Jessica was doing, but she knew there was no way he'd let her set foot in the Superstitions without him.

Fighting back a grin, she dismounted. "We'll stop here for a break. There's a small spring in those rocks where you can refill your canteens."

"Well, it's about time," Charlie muttered as he stiffly climbed down from his horse and surveyed their surroundings with a jaundiced eye. His snort of contempt said it all.

Alex silently echoed the older man's opinion, an impatient frown darkening his brow as his eyes met Jessica's. They'd been moving at a snail's pace for hours now. If she took a break every time they covered a couple of miles, Harlan would be dead and buried before he found the money and got back. "We can take a break at lunch," he said autocratically. "Let's push on."

She wasn't a woman prone to violence, Jessica reminded herself as she looked up at Alex. But some people didn't know when they were pushing their luck. She and Mr. Trent were going to get a few things settled right now!

Stepping closer to his horse, she gave him a saccharine smile guaranteed to infuriate him. "You're paying me a lot of money to lead this little expedition," she reminded him sweetly. "And that means I'm in charge. *We're* taking a break."

Charlie and Slim exchanged knowing grins at her tone, but Alex never dragged his eyes away from Jessica. When was the last time he'd met a woman who got under his skin? That willful light in her eyes irritated the hell out of him, and if he'd had the time he'd have done something about it.

Like drag her into his arms and kiss her until she couldn't think straight.

He scowled. Where the hell had that come from? The lady wasn't his type. He liked his women soft, sophisticated, sweet-smelling. Not lean and tough, with a razor-sharp tongue and smelling of dust and horses. He'd do well to remember that.

The look he gave her was one that had been known to set his victims on the witness stand quaking. "And if I disagree?"

Outwardly, Jessica never flinched, but inside she was cringing. "You'll go on alone," she answered promptly, refusing to be intimidated. "But I wouldn't advise it. Not unless you want to die of heatstroke the first day."

She was right, of course. This was her playground, he reminded himself, forcing himself to relax. He'd let her set the rules. For now. But if she thought she was going to win every argument so easily, she was in for a rude awakening. "All right," he shrugged, his smile just the faintest bit dangerous as he slowly dismounted. "We'll do things your way."

Somehow, that smile didn't reassure her. "Don't tell me you're giving in so easily. I'm disappointed."

"Don't push your luck. Quit while you're ahead."

His low growl slid down her spine, trailing a shiver of awareness in its wake. "We'll take a twenty-minute break," she told him coolly, then turned on her heel to head for the spring.

This time he'd let her have the last word, Alex thought as he watched her go down on her knees beside the small pool, which was almost concealed by the rocks. She splashed water onto her face, gasping at its coolness. He couldn't stop his eyes from running over her slender hips encased in jeans and the gentle swell of her breasts curving against the soft white cotton of her blouse. He swore softly, unable to stop looking at her. All he'd wanted was a guide to take him into the mountains, someone who wouldn't ask too many questions or interfere with what he had to do. What he'd gotten instead was a woman who took every opportunity to infuriate him. The next few days were going to be long ones.

Jessica, settling in the shade of an outcropping of rock, silently echoed his thoughts. Alex Trent obviously had a problem with taking orders from a woman, and she'd just have to develop a little patience. Only patience had never been one of her strong suits, she reflected ruefully. If they got through the next few days without coming to blows, it would be a minor miracle.

They started out again twenty minutes later, with Jessica in the lead and Charlie once again in the rear. They left the trail almost immediately, abandoning its clearly marked outline for one that was barely discernible. Without warning, the going became treacherous. They skirted an unexpected ravine that seemed to drop off into infinity before it gave way to the jagged rocks that waited for the unwary at the bottom. The Superstitions made no allowances for carelessness.

The pace slowed to a crawl, but Jessica didn't even notice that Alex made no objection. Her jaw was set grimly, and it took all her concentration to keep her hands light on the reins. She deliberately kept her mind empty of the memories pushing at her, and her eyes were trained on the rocky ground directly in front of her mare. She didn't realize she was holding her breath until she released it in a shaky sigh as she entered the hidden canyon she and her grandfather had stumbled across when she'd been twelve.

For a long, tense moment she sat ummoving, her heart pounding, and waited for the others to catch up. She had to get a grip, she told herself sternly. The mountains had nearly destroyed her once before. She'd be damned if she'd let them get to her again.

Alex whistled softly as he drew up beside her, his eyes on the stark magnificence of their surroundings. Sheer cliffs rose sharply from the narrow canyon floor, dark, slick, dangerous. There seemed to be no break in the rock walls, the only outlet the way they had come. Overhead, the jagged crown of the mountains cast a silent, eerie silhouette against the brilliance of the sun.

Civilization suddenly seemed a world away.

Alex turned to Jessica, and raised a dark brow inquiringly. "It looks like a box canyon."

"Looks are deceiving up here," she warned softly. "Nothing's as it appears."

Alex's mustache twitched. "More superstitions, Jessica?"

She shrugged. "Maybe, maybe not. There's been strange stories about these mountains ever since Coronado mysteriously lost some of his conquistadores hundreds of years ago. More than one man has come up here and never been seen again.''

That he could believe, he thought as he stared at the empty terrain. It was a land fit only for spiders and snakes, with one canyon looking much like another. A man could make a wrong turn and not know until it was too late. Pulling off his hat, he wiped the sweat from his face and glared at the sun. ''If there's a killer up here, it's not the mountains. It's that damn sun. It's hotter than hell.''

''No.'' Jessica chuckled. ''Right now it's just warm. This afternoon it'll be hot!''

''That's what I'm afraid of,'' Alex groaned. Then he frowned at the gravel that suddenly bounced and slid down the nearest cliff. He glanced up, and every muscle in his body seemed to freeze in horror. A huge boulder was rolling down the cliff at breakneck speed. Jessica and her horse were right in its path.

''Look out!'' he cried hoarsely as he sprang from his horse to hers. He slammed into her, hardly hearing her cry of surprise and pain as he dragged her to the ground. Her horse bolted, and a heartbeat later the boulder landed with a sickening crash.

For what seemed like an eternity, no one moved. Alex covered Jessica with his body, pressing her into the ground, his arms like steel bands around her. A rock bruised her back, and a bump was already rising on her head from the force of her landing, but she didn't even notice. Numbly she stared at the huge rock now sitting squarely in the middle of the path.

It could have killed her horse, she thought dazedly. It could have killed her.

Visions of her husband's death rose up to haunt her, and it was then that the coldness started—a biting, sinister cold that defied the heat and defied the reassuring warmth of the hard male body cradling her close. It chilled her very soul. She told herself that Derrick's death had been caused by a fall; the two situations weren't even remotely similiar. But fear didn't listen to reason. A shiver ran down her spine with icy fingers, and suddenly she couldn't stop shaking.

Alex's arms tightened instinctively; his breath was still tearing through his lungs. God, that was close. Too close. If he'd jumped a second later, she wouldn't have had a chance. He didn't want to think what that boulder would have done to her. "Are you all right?" he asked huskily.

She nodded against his chest, not realizing she was clutching him in a death grip. "I—I'm f-fine."

Alex drew back far enough to see her face. Like hell she was fine! Her hair tumbled past her shoulders, and there wasn't a drop of color in her face. She was shaking like a leaf. He scowled. "Are you sure you're not hurt? That was a pretty hard fall you took."

"Jessie, girl, are you hurt?" Charlie threw himself from his horse and rushed to her side. He'd seen the rock barreling toward her the minute he'd followed Slim into the canyon, but time had suddenly slipped into slow motion and he hadn't been able to get to her fast enough. "Damn it, girl, speak to me! Are you hurt?"

"Give her time to get her breath," Slim said quietly as he gazed at Jessica in concern. "She's awfully pale."

"It's these damn mountains," Charlie growled. "I knew she shouldn't have come back up here. We ought to turn around right now and head for the ranch."

Alex moved to gather her into his arms, his eyes filled with worry. "Let me get her out of this damn sun, and we'll rest."

"No!" Jessica struggled to her feet, pushing out of Alex's arms. Panic gave her the strength she needed to stand on her own. She couldn't accept their concern, their sympathy, not now. She was too vulnerable, the horror of the past too close. Couldn't they see that one kind word was all it would take to push her into tears? "I'm fine," she insisted in a voice that wasn't quite as strong as she'd have liked. "Don't take a break on my account."

"Yeah, you look fine," Charlie replied angrily. "You're as white as a ghost. And you ought to be. These damn mountains nearly killed you."

Alex stifled a grin, relieved to see the color flood back into Jessica's cheeks when she glared at the old man. So he wasn't the only male she raised that chin to. Picking up her hat, he stepped to her side and handed it to her, then reached for her wild mane with both hands. He felt her start in surprise, but his fingers were lost in the silky softness of the ebony strands. With a gentle twist, he piled it on top of her head, then took her hat back and plopped it over the dark mass. His eyes locked with hers as his fingers slowly slid down her neck and over her shoulders. "Charlie's right," he said huskily, pulling away. "That was a close call. Sure you don't want to rest for a few minutes?"

For just a moment, Jessica couldn't think, let alone speak. What kind of magic did this man have in his hands? she wondered, horrified. How could he make her skin tingle with just a touch? Drawing in a sharp breath, she moved away from him abruptly, deliberately ignoring the sudden rush of heat in her blood. "It was just a freak accident," she said tightly. "Let's forget it. I'm fine."

Her withdrawal wasn't lost on him. His eyes glinted dangerously. "Tomorrow you'll be black and blue from that fall."

"You're wasting your time, Alex," Charlie told him in disgust. "Once she makes up her mind, she's stubborn as a mule." Shaking his head, he headed for his horse. "Women!"

Grinning, Slim handed Jessica the reins to her horse. "Here you go, Jessie. Want me to help you up?"

"No—"

"I'll do it," Alex cut in. Her gaze flew to his in alarm, drawing a grin from him. "Since I knocked you off, the least I can do is help you back up."

"No, I don't need any help," she began, but it was too late. He was behind her, his hands settling at her waist. A mistake, she thought in growing panic. Letting this man touch her was a mistake. She glanced over her shoulder to tell him she was perfectly capable of mounting the horse by herself, but somehow the words died in her throat. She felt her heart drop to her knees and could do nothing to stop it. Deep inside her the shaking started again, but this time it had nothing to do with fear and everything to do with the man who held her captive so easily.

Alex's fingers tightened. So she felt it, too, he thought with a frown. The sparks, the heat, the *need*. Damn it, where had it come from? Desire wasn't new to him, but he'd never felt it this fast, this fiercely. Especially for a woman he wasn't even sure he liked! From the look in her eyes, she didn't want these feelings any more than he did.

So what was he going to do about it? he wondered as he helped her up into the saddle. Nothing. Absolutely nothing.

All that day and the next they moved deeper into the mountains, traversing gaping ravines and narrow ledges where one false step could lead to eternity. The sun followed their halting progress, tracking them relentlessly. Its burning rays made a mockery of their protective clothing and sunscreen. By the time they stopped to make camp the second night, they were bone-weary, sunburned and covered with dust from the trail. They ate a cold supper and retired before it was dark, thankful for the sleeping bags when the night abruptly turned chilly. By dawn they were once again on their way.

The heat, the dust and the slow pace they were forced to maintain had tempers straining. Jessica struggled to keep her cool, but if Alex Trent argued with her about one more thing she was going to blow up! He'd stopped complaining about the slow pace, but that didn't stop him from challenging her at every turn—sometimes without saying a word.

It was that mocking look of his, she decided irritably. All he had to do was lift a brow and she wanted to kick him!

Urging her mare up a steep, rocky incline, she frowned as she heard Alex softly encourage his own horse to follow hers. She was entirely too aware of him, and she didn't like it.

Granted, he was a handsome devil, but he was also impossibly arrogant, domineering, infuriating—the type of man that women leaned on. And loved. She scowled at the thought. The women in Phoenix might fall all over him when he flashed his dimples, but she was determined not to be impressed. She couldn't allow herself to forget that he was after the Lost Dutchman. That was more damning than all his other faults put together. She could handle his arrogance, but she wanted nothing to do with a man who believed in fairy tales. Satisfied that she had finally worked out her emotions where Alex Trent was concerned, Jessica pulled her mare to a stop at the top of the ridge they'd been climbing for the past hour. A slow grin spread across her face at the sight of the low-hanging trees off to her right. They had finally arrived!

"This is it," she told the others as they caught up with her. "There's a series of springs under those trees. We'll set up camp there."

She started to nudge her horse forward, but Alex's hand shot out and grabbed her reins. "Wait a minute," he growled, the expression in his gaze hard as it met hers. "If I read that map correctly, the springs are quite a ways from where we'll be digging."

Jessica nodded. "The arch you're looking for is about a half a mile from here. Over there," she said, gesturing to the left.

"Then we'll camp there," he said flatly.

"And carry water in this heat? Thanks, but no thanks. We'll camp at the springs."

Alex struggled to hang on to his patience, but it was hard. "Look," he said in exasperation, "I intend to keep my eye on the digging site, and I can't do that from a half a mile away. Since I'm paying for this little expedition, I'm calling the shots from here on out. We'll camp at the rocks."

"*You* can camp anywhere you like," she countered, anger flushing her cheeks. No one gave her orders! "When you need us, you'll find us at the springs."

So she was calling a Mexican standoff. His eyes swept over her slim figure, noting the delicacy of her build, the softness of her skin—and the stubborn set of her jaw. He swore softly. "Are you one of those women who always insists on having her own way because you feel threatened by a man?''

If he'd expected outrage, she thought, he was disappointed. There was hurt, stronger than she liked, but she'd have died before she'd have let him see it. A cold smile flirted with her mouth as she studied him openly. When her gaze came back to his, Alex had the distinct impression she found him lacking somehow. ''Are you one of those men who's always throwing his weight around just to prove you're a man?''

''I've got other ways of proving I'm a man,'' he retorted. ''Just say the word and I'll be happy to show them to you.''

''Whoa, whoa!'' Charlie laughed, recognizing the storm clouds gathering in Jessica's eyes. ''End of round one, and I'd say it's a draw. Now are we going to set up camp before dark or sit here yapping all night?''

Silence, cold and tense, was his only answer. ''You could set up camp halfway between,'' Slim finally suggested quietly. ''The walk to the springs would only be half as far, but you could still see the digging site.''

It was a reasonable compromise. ''We'd still have to haul water,'' Jessica said stiffly, ''but I suppose I can live with it. How 'bout you, Alex?''

Proud and unbending to the very end, Alex thought. ''I'm a reasonable man. As long as I get my way.'' He grinned.

"I don't believe it," Charlie muttered. "You two are actually agreeing on something. Let's set up camp before you change your minds."

They arranged the four tents in a semicircle in the center of an area relatively clear of rocks. The ring of hammers against metal stakes echoed in the clear air. Caught up in their work, they didn't even notice when the sun slipped behind the mountains and the sky turned crimson. The air slowly cooled, and from the rocks near the spring, two quail called to each other. Twilight turned to dusk.

Making a final check on the last tent, Jessica straightened and pressed a hand to her lower back as exhaustion seeped into her bones. Her eyes lifted to the deepening shadows of the mountains. It would be night soon, and when the darkness came it would drop like a shroud. On a moonless night like tonight, the dangers would be greater than usual. The stygian blackness cleverly concealed waiting hazards, drop offs, death.

Shutting out the painful memories, she straightened her weary shoulders and determinedly moved to the nearest pack horse. As long as she kept busy she couldn't think of her surroundings or the past.

"As soon as we get the rest of this stuff unpacked, the horses need to be watered and fed. Slim, I'll leave that to you." She reached for a box of cooking equipment. "We need to get lanterns filled and lit before it's too dark to see. And see about supper—"

"I'll do that," Charlie said quickly. "I know better than to let you anywhere near a campfire."

Alex watched her sag under the heavy weight of the box and moved to her side in two quick, angry strides. What was she trying to prove? "Give me that," he growled, taking it before she could protest. "Where do you want it?"

"Over there," she snapped, her eyes flashing in the growing darkness. She pointed to a flat rock that would serve well as a table. "But I could have done it myself."

"I never doubted it for a minute. I just thought you were in a hurry to start supper before dark."

"Oh, no," Charlie said. "She's not doing the cooking. I am." At Alex's look of surprise, a slow grin spread across Charlie's weathered face. "Jessie's not real fond of cooking. Somehow she just never seemed to get the hang of it. Not that she didn't try," he quickly added with a chuckle. "But she knew it was hopeless when she made gravy and one of the hands used it for wallpaper paste."

"And it worked," Slim chimed, a rare smile tugging at his mouth. "That paper's still up in the bunkhouse."

Long used to being teased about her disasters in the kitchen, Jessica only laughed. "I ruined a skillet making that gravy. It stuck so bad I had to throw it out. And it was one of Mary Lou's favorite pans." She shook her head ruefully. "She wouldn't let me near the kitchen after that."

Fascinated in spite of himself, Alex watched a tantalizing mixture of amusement and memories play across Jessica's face. Her laughter, quick and husky, slipped into his blood, heating it. Suddenly he wanted her in his arms, her mouth soft and pliant under his.

Don't be a fool, he thought in disgust, abruptly turning away to set the box where she'd indicated. Beneath that beautiful exterior was a wildcat who'd probably spit and scratch at the touch of a man's hands.

"I'm going to look for some wood near the springs," she said as she took one of the lanterns Charlie was filling and lighted it. "We'll need some kindling to get the fire started."

"I'll go with you." The words were out before Alex could stop them. He didn't like the idea of her wandering around in the dark by herself. Cursing under his breath, he met her look of surprise with a shrug. "I need to stretch my legs."

Jessica studied him shrewdly, seeing through his excuse in an instant. What was she going to do? He was as overprotective as Charlie. Torn between irritation and amusement, she sighed. "I don't need a baby-sitter to watch over me, Alex. I'm a big girl. Charlie will tell you I'm perfectly capable of taking care of myself."

The words were barely out of her mouth when a dark, sinister figure silently stepped out of the darkness.

Chapter 4

The light from the lantern picked him out of the darkness. He was built like the mountains—tall, rough. His eyes were as black as ebony in a face that was totally lacking in softness. He carried no weapon, but both his size and the way he had silently materialized were threatening.

Jessica froze. Her heart pounded. Damn it, where were their rifles? Glancing around wildly, she spied them over by the tents, carelessly propped against the rocks, out of reach. She swore softly. Of all the asinine things to do! One of the first things her grandfather had taught her about the mountains was to always keep her rifle close. Danger had a habit of creeping up on you if you weren't prepared.

Alex also spotted the weapons, their barrels gleaming dully in the dim light. The expression in his eyes turned hard and dangerous as he gauged the distance at about thirty feet. Their visitor might not have a gun, but for all Alex knew he could have a few friends hiding out in the darkness armed to the teeth. He'd feel a hell of a lot safer with a rifle in his hand.

He started to ease from Jessica's side, but he'd hardly taken a step when the man standing at the edge of darkness shattered the tense silence. "You aren't wanted here," he stated in a cold, flat voice that was all the more dangerous for its softness. "Go home while you still can."

In the next instant he was gone as silently as he'd come, disappearing back into the night. Stunned, Jessica looked from the empty darkness to her companions. Charlie strode over to the rifles and tossed one to each of them before snatching up his own. "From now on, this baby goes everywhere I go. Damn mountains. I knew we shouldn't have come."

"I think I'll make sure our friend really left," Alex said grimly, striding toward the spot where they'd last seen the Indian. "We don't want any more surprises tonight."

"Wait!" Jessica cried in alarm, but he'd already been swallowed up in the cloak of darkness. "Damn it," she called after him in frustration. "Don't blame me if you fall off a cliff. You're not taking a walk in the park, you know!"

His laughter drifted back to her. "And I didn't think you cared. I'm touched."

"If these mountains don't kill him, I think I will," she muttered, glaring out at the black night.

"If you still want that wood," Charlie said from behind her, "I'll go with you."

To protect her. Charlie acted as if she were as unfamiliar with the mountains as Alex Trent! Turning to face the older man, she struggled to hold on to her patience. "I'm the one who knows these mountains, remember? Nothing's going to happen to me between here and the springs."

"Never figured it would," the older man stated flatly. "Just thought I'd help you carry the wood. Course, if you don't want my help..."

Jessica fought back a smile at his wounded tone. The crafty old goat. Who did he think he was fooling? She picked up the lantern. "Well, in that case, let's get going."

When Alex returned to the camp less than fifteen minutes later, a small fire was burning brightly, fighting off the surrounding darkness. For just a moment, he allowed himself to appreciate the peacefulness of the scene. A battered black pot hung over the campfire, and the scent of freeze-dried stew drifted on the clear night air. On the other side of the tents, Slim was brushing the horses with slow, methodical strokes. Jessica and Charlie sat on the ground near the fire, each using a convenient boulder as a backrest as they talked quietly.

It could have been a scene right out of the Old West. Right down to the rifles they were cleaning.

Frowning, Alex stepped into the circle of light. "I lost him," he said when they looked up in alarm. "Just when I thought I was on to him, he vanished. I circled back just to make sure he'd really gone, but I'm damned if I know where he went."

Charlie leaned his rifle against a rock and moved to the fire to stir the stew. A cigar was stuck in the corner of his mouth. "Ain't surprised," he muttered. "The Indians were here long before the rest of us. If anyone knows the mountains' secrets, they do. And if we had any sense, we'd head back for the ranch at first light."

"You're not taking that warning seriously?" Alex scoffed as he squatted next to Jessica. "This is a national wilderness area. We've got just as much right to be here as anyone else."

"The Indians don't always see it that way," the older man argued. "Especially when someone wanders onto their sacred ground. From what Jessie tells me, we're smack-dab in the middle of it." As he leaned over the fire, his sharp green eyes lifted to the dark, silent mountains that seemed to hover over them threateningly. "I can remember people talking about the Apaches and their thunder god when I was a kid. Course, life out here was a lot wilder then, and only a fool looking for trouble came into the mountains, but those legends still mean a mighty lot to some people."

"My grandfather used to say that there was always trouble brewing when a storm hit the mountains," Jessica added quietly, her hands on her rifle, her blue eyes dark with remembrance. "The old thunder god would throw lightning with one hand, stir up the wind with the other and thunder with rage if anyone dared to displease him. To appease him, the Apaches swore vengeance on anyone who violated his sacred home."

Slim quietly joined them, a frown furrowing his brow. "Think that guy was Apache?"

Jessica shrugged. "Probably. Though there are other tribes in this area—the Pimas, the Maricopas—and these mountains are sacred to them, too."

"You really think they'd cause trouble if they got the chance?" Alex asked, unable to believe they were taking a bunch of superstitions so seriously.

"It wouldn't be the first time," Charlie said grimly. "A lot of strange things have happened up here. Disappearances, murder, you name it. Men have been known to lose their heads here. Literally."

Jessica shivered, her fingers unconsciously gripping her rifle as old pain, long since buried, stirred restlessly. A moment of terror ripped out of time mocked her, reminding her all too clearly just how vicious the mountains could be. She swallowed, suddenly pale. She should never have come back.

Jumping to her feet, she deliberately changed the subject. "That stew's bound to be ready by now. Let's eat."

They ate quietly, lost in their own thoughts. Her appetite nonexistent, Jessica tried in vain to shake off the bad memories and the uneasiness gripping her. The night was inky, opaque, concealing. For the last two days she'd frequently felt as if someone were watching them, but never so strongly as now. It was, she knew, a feeling peculiar to the mountains. For as long as she could remember, they'd always been silent, watchful, waiting.

And they were obviously intolerant of intruders, she thought uneasily. Setting her half-full plate aside, she rose and stepped closer to the campfire, suddenly cold.

Surprised, Alex watched the firelight play off the delicate lines of her face. She was pale, nervous. He hadn't thought she was a woman prone to nervousness. "Maybe we should post a watch tonight. Just in case."

"Wouldn't hurt," Charlie agreed, peering out into the darkness. "It's awful quiet out there."

Alex silently agreed. It was the type of quiet he was all too familiar with. The type that settled over back alleys and dark streets right before trouble broke out. Where it would come from, or when, was anyone's guess. He planned to be ready.

Taking his empty plate over to the worktable, he glanced back over his shoulder at Charlie and Slim. "Who wants to take first watch?"

They both shrugged, indicating it made no difference to them. Jessica bristled. They hadn't even bothered to pretend to include her in the conversation. Well, she wouldn't leave the job of protecting to the men.

"*I'll* take the first watch," she said determinedly.

Charlie and Slim knew better than to argue with her when she spoke in that tone. Alex frowned. "There's no need for you to do that, not when there are three men here.''

Charlie winced, then shared a grin with Slim as they sat back to wait for the fireworks. "Oh, boy, you've done it now," he muttered.

"You certainly have," Jessica retorted, her eyes flashing as she advanced until she was only inches away from him. "I don't know what kind of women you've been hanging around, Mr. Trent, but not all of us like to be wrapped in cotton while the men take care of everything. Especially me. I can take care of myself. So if you want more trouble than you can handle, just try treating me like a helpless woman again," she dared him, lifting her chin.

Alex grinned. Damn, she was magnificent when she was angry. The passion was there, straining at her control. What would it take to set it free? Before he left these mountains, he was going to find out.

Ignoring the two men who were watching them so closely, he leaned closer, gazing at her mouth before slowly, reluctantly meeting her eyes. "I haven't begun to treat you like a woman," he growled huskily. "When I do, I can guarantee you won't complain."

Her eyes narrowed. "Don't hold your breath," she advised him coolly. "It'll never happen."

A dark brow arched. "Wanna bet?"

She bit back a quick denial, unable to drag her eyes away from the sensuous curve of his mouth beneath his mustache. He was a man who would know how to please a woman. The thought slipped into her consciousness, teasing her, tempting her, horrifying her.

Nothing in her life had prepared her for Alex Trent. Still, she'd never turned her back on a dare, and she wasn't about to start now. She threw caution to the winds and hoped she wouldn't live to regret it. If he wanted a battle of wills, she'd be more than happy to give him one. "Name the stakes."

"I'll wait till I win." He stuck out his hand, his grin wicked. "Deal?"

She was playing with fire. Even as the thought came to her, she was giving him her hand. "Deal." A pact with the devil, she thought wildly as she saw the triumphant light in his eyes. She'd made a pact with the devil himself, and it was too late to back out. Fighting her rising panic, she hastily withdrew her hand. She turned to find Charlie and Slim struggling with the need to grin. "I'll take the first watch." This time no one argued.

Forty-five minutes later the supper dishes had been cleaned, the three men had retired to their tents and quiet had descended on the camp. Jessica sat propped up against a rock, her rifle at her side, and stared at the tent Alex had taken. Right next to hers.

Her blue eyes clouded with frustration. What had possessed her to make that bet with him? He was arrogant, overprotective and too damn charming for his own good. When he smiled his mischievous grin, she found herself wanting, *needing*, to taste his mouth. It was crazy. She'd actually dared him to try to make love to her.

She didn't doubt for a minute that he'd try. He'd enjoy every second, and she had a horrible feeling he could make her enjoy it, too.

But she didn't want a man in her life. She had too many already—Charlie, her sons, not to mention a whole ranchful of cowboys who made no secret of the fact that they thought she should stay out of the heat and let the men do the work. She wanted nothing to do with Alex Trent!

Deliberately turning away from the tents, she wrapped her arms around her legs and rested her chin on her knees. Her gaze shifted to the cliffs, just out of reach of the campfire's dying light. From out of the darkness, the trill of a mockingbird suddenly shattered the heavy silence that had shrouded the mountains all day. Suddenly the night was alive with furtive sounds. She heard a rustle, the sigh of a breeze and, far off in the distance, the cry of a coyote echoing hauntingly through the surrounding canyons.

Tension crawled up Jessica's spine with icy fingers that slowly, persistently tightened her nerves. It was just the mountains, she told herself firmly, and tried to believe it. The wildlife that hid from the deadly rays of the sun during the day was coming out. There was no one out there, no one watching her.

Near the tents, the sudden sound of a booted foot on the rocky ground was like a gunshot.

Her heart in her throat, Jessica snatched up her gun and whirled, her rifle cocked and ready.

Alex lifted his hands, his grin wry, irritation flickering in his eyes. This was getting to be a habit! "Do you sleep with that thing, too?"

She sent him a withering glance and set the rifle down again, well within reach. "You're going to get shot sneaking up on people that way. Especially up here."

Her gaze returned to their surroundings, so she didn't see Alex's quick frown. For just a moment, the expression in her eyes had been unguarded, exposed, vulnerable, and it had caught him off guard. He started forward, the need to reassure her strong within him, only to stop when he realized what he was doing. His imagination was playing tricks on him! Jessica Rawlins could stand toe-to-toe with the devil himself and spit in his eye. She didn't want or need any man's protection, and he'd be wise to remember that.

Why, then, did he still have the crazy desire to go to her and wrap her in his arms? To just hold her? She'd probably come up swinging.

Grinning at the thought, he strode over to the fire and took a place beside her, his eyes teasing. "Seen any bogeymen?"

"Just you."

Alex laughed. The lady had a sharp tongue. "No roars of disapproval from the thunder god?" he probed. "No flashes of lightning? I'm disappointed."

His arrogance never ceased to amaze her. "I hope you're still laughing by the time we get out of here," she said dryly.

"Don't you mean *if* I get out of here? The thunder god may decide to toss me off a cliff once we start digging up his sacred ground."

"Don't say that!"

Alex watched in surprise at her stricken face. "I was just kidding," he said quietly. "Surely you don't believe all that mumbo jumbo? I thought you were too practical to fall for a bunch of tales dreamed up by the local chamber of commerce to bring in tourists."

"Damn it, no one dreamed up anything!" she snapped, jumping to her feet to pace agitatedly. "It's these mountains. They do funny things to your mind, and before you know it you're doing things you'd normally never do. Men have wandered away from their camps and never come back. Others have come up here for a vacation and stayed, forgetting their families, their jobs, their responsibilities. And others," she said huskily, her eyes haunted, "have died." She stared out into the darkness. "I hate it up here."

Her words were fierce and full of pain. Alex stood and followed her to the edge of the darkness, stopping just short of touching her. His eyes touched her dark hair drawn back in a ponytail, the nape of her neck, the curve of her cheek. "Why?" he asked softly. "Why do you hate the mountains?"

"Because they've tried to take everything I ever loved." The resentment went back to her childhood, but it had taken Derrick's death to turn the resentment to hatred. "My grandfather was one of those souls seduced by the mountains. They lured him up here with promises of gold, and he was too weak to resist. He'd come up here for weeks at a time and leave me to run the ranch. Even when he did come home, the mountains were here, waiting for him.''

Alex frowned. ''You talk about them as if they're alive.''

''They are,'' she said simply, turning to face him. ''Don't ever make the mistake of trusting them. Men have died for less.''

Something in her tone twisted his guts. ''Someone you know?''

She nodded once, her face expressionless. ''My husband.''

Alex automatically reached for her. He squeezed her shoulder in apology. ''God, Jessica, I should have realized. I'm sorry.''

''So am I,'' she said simply. Sorry that he'd died so young, so tragically, without ever knowing she was pregnant. Sorry for all the years she'd been too busy to dwell on the past. But most of all she was sorry that the memories of her marriage were wrapped in the cotton-candy daydreams of a teenager hovering on the edge of womanhood. She had three sons by a man whose smile she could hardly remember.

Shifting emotions passed across her blue eyes. Everything in Alex warned him to leave her pain, her memories, *her*, alone. But he'd never been one to listen to warnings. His fingers tightened ever so slightly. ''Jessica . . .''

She glanced up and found herself caught in the intensity of his gaze. There was sympathy there, and something else, something dark and dangerous and so infinitely tempting that just for a moment it threatened to weaken her knees. He was too close. The camp was quiet, and the surrounding darkness trapped them in the firelight. She knew she should move, preferably to the other side of the world. Maybe then she'd feel safe from the feelings this man stirred in her so effortlessly.

Suddenly aware of where her thoughts had wandered without her consent, she stepped back. "Aren't you supposed to be sleeping?"

"I couldn't," he explained, moving closer to the fire and putting another piece of their meager supply of wood on the dying flames. "Too quiet, I guess." He glanced back at her silent figure, and the firelight seemed to glow in the depths of his hazel eyes. "Your watch is just about up, anyway. Why don't you go on to bed?"

She almost laughed at the suggestion. Her mind was a mass of conflicting thoughts and unwanted memories, and her body still trembled from the longings he'd stirred in her with just a look. How could she possibly sleep?

"I think I'll sit up awhile," she said. "I'm wide awake."

They settled before the fire without another word, Jessica on one side and Alex on the other, neither willing to break the silence that suddenly enveloped them. Her legs drawn up beneath her, Jessica settled back against her rock. She gazed at the hypnotizing dance of the campfire. Before she realized it, the lateness and her exhaustion caught up with her and pulled her into sleep.

Alex watched as her head drifted down to her shoulder, just barely able to resist the urge to go to her and ease her into a more comfortable position. She fell asleep with the quickness of a child, he thought in amusement. His smile slowly faded as his eyes roamed freely over her. Dark tendrils of hair that had escaped the confines of her ponytail swept the curve of her cheek, giving her a look of vulnerability she would have despised. She tried so hard to conceal her femininity beneath her jeans and her work shirts and her bossy attitude, but she couldn't hide the softness of her skin, the sweet, sensuous curve of her mouth, the willowy suppleness of her body.

Heat kicked into his stomach. His eyes were drawn to the curve of her breast, the smallness of her waist and her impossibly long legs. No, he silently corrected himself, she was no child. She was a woman made for a man's hands. She was passion waiting to be tapped.

Did she still grieve for her dead husband?

His jaw hardened at the thought, and irritation glittered in his eyes. He was getting entirely too interested in Jessica Rawlins, and it had to stop right now. He had no business thinking twice about a woman like her. She was stubborn, temperamental and too used to getting her way. If that wasn't enough, she came with three kids, a ranch and a bunch of overprotective cowboys who'd probably string him up if they knew how easily he pictured her in his bed.

What the hell was the matter with him? he wondered, glaring at her sleeping form. He'd seen her kind before. She had commitment written all over her, and he didn't doubt for a minute that she could tie a man in knots before he knew what hit him. He wasn't standing still and letting any women do that to him.

Jumping to his feet, he strode quickly around the fire and leaned down to shake her awake. At the feel of the pliancy of her sleeping body his jaw clenched, and his tone was sharper than he realized. "Jessica? C'mon, wake up. You'll get a crick in your neck from sleeping like that."

She blinked, confused, a frown knitting her brow at the sight of his scowling face so close to hers. "What?"

"It's late." He released her and abruptly straightened to his full height to glower down at her. "If you don't go to bed, you'll be so stiff tomorrow you won't be able to move."

"All right, all right, I'm going," she muttered as she scrambled to her feet, her blue eyes dark with resentment. "You don't have to get hateful about it."

"You should be in bed."

"You're right about that," she retorted coldly, snatching up her rifle. "My bed's back at the ranch. I wish to God I was in it." She stormed off to her tent without a backward glance.

Alex watched her every step of the way. She was trouble with a capital *T* and he was glad she'd finally left. Why then, he wondered furiously, did he have an

insane desire to go after her and kiss her senseless? It
must be the damn mountains. She'd warned him they
could do funny things to his mind.

Sighing, he turned back to the campfire to con-
tinue his watch.

Chapter 5

The sun was spilling over the jagged edge of the mountains when the party left camp on foot and walked the short distance to where Alex had indicated he intended to dig. No longer needing the map to guide her, Jessica stopped short at the sight of a rockslide that had cut off the end of the canyon. The last time she'd been in the canyon there had been a small natural arch carved out of the side of the cliff, a product of centuries of wind and rain. That arch was what Alex had sought, but it was now at their feet—a thousand pounds of rubble and broken boulders.

Pushing her hat to the back of her head, she surveyed the mess in disgust. "This is it," she told Alex.

"Or at least what's left of it. Too bad. It was a nice arch."

He glanced at her sharply. "Are you sure? It's easy to get confused up here—everything looks alike. Maybe we're in the wrong canyon."

Jessica dragged in an indignant breath and told herself to hang on to her patience. But it was hard, especially when she'd spent most of the night trying to get Alex out of her head. She said carefully, "No, Alex, we're not in the wrong canyon. There was only one arch in these mountains, and it was on that canyon wall. If you'll look at your map, you'll see we're in the right place."

He knew she was right, and he stared at the pile of rocks in frustration. Harlan had hidden the money in a cave under that arch and then closed the entrance with a small blast of dynamite. The old man had assured him that it wouldn't take more than a half day's digging to uncover the cave. With Slim and Charlie to help with the excavation, Alex had figured it would take even less time.

He should have known it wouldn't be that easy. It would take days, possibly weeks, to dig out the two-story pile of rock that now covered the cave entrance. Damn it, he didn't have that kind of time!

"Well," Jessica said, "this obviously isn't what you expected to find. What do you want to do?"

"We dig," he said flatly. "I'm not leaving till I get what I came for."

She looked at him as if he'd lost his mind. "You've got to be kidding! You can't really believe that the

Lost Dutchman is buried under all those rocks. Even if the damn mine does exist, it's supposed to be miles from here.''

Aware that Charlie and Slim were listening to every word, Alex stifled the urge to tell her what he was really looking for. ''Why did you agree to bring me up here if you didn't really think I'd find anything?'' he asked instead.

''Because I need the money.''

The guilt that nagged him every time she mentioned the Lost Dutchman vanished. He couldn't tell her about the stolen cash, not yet. He didn't doubt for a minute that he could trust her with his life, but he wasn't so sure about the money. The need for money could do strange things to people.

Handing her a pick, he said, ''It'll take us days to get through all this. If it'll help the work seem easier, just think of all the money you're going to make.''

For nearly three days they worked in the broiling-hot sun, cursing the heat, the grime, the sweat that stung their eyes and the rocks that cut their fingers and burned their palms. The boulders that they couldn't move they broke apart with picks, venting their frustrations with every blow. It was backbreaking work, made even worse by the unrelenting rays of the sun. The canyon trapped the heat like a giant oven, baking them alive. Charlie swore that hell would be a picnic by comparison. Alex had to agree.

Through it all, Jessica worked alongside the men, never issuing a word of complaint. She was lifting and shoving and doing what had to be done, ignoring the tiredness that made her bones ache.

Taking a much-needed break late in the afternoon of the third day, Alex stood in the shade of a boulder and watched as she fanned herself with her hat. Loose strands of her dark hair clung to Jessica's face. Her yellow blouse was damp against her breasts, her cheeks tinged with sunburn. Dirt and sweat shouldn't look good on a woman, he thought annoyed. And she was too beautiful for his peace of mind.

Cursing the Fates, he reached for his canteen and took a swig of water, determined to ignore Jessica. But he'd been trying that for three days, ever since they'd started digging, and the situation was only getting worse. How could he ignore her when she was there at every turn, doing her share of the work with a strength and grittiness he couldn't help but admire? It was irritating. If they didn't get out of these mountains soon, he was going to be in big trouble!

He clenched his jaw and screwed the canteen cap back on. Shooting a sharp glance at the others he asked, "Ready?"

Jessica plopped her hat back on her head by way of an answer and headed for the large boulder she and Alex had been chiseling at before the break. "Come on, guys." She laughed when she heard Charlie and Slim groan in unison as they got to their feet. "A couple more hours and we can quit—"

The shot came out of nowhere, a sharp cracking sound that split the mountain stillness and landed with a thud not three feet from where she stood. She stared dumbly at the dust kicked up by the bullet.

For what seemed like an eternity, nobody moved. In the next instant there was another crack, and all hell broke loose. Charlie and Slim dived for cover and their guns, while Alex caught Jessica around the hips in a low, diving tackle, rolling her behind a rock that wasn't nearly as large as he'd have liked. Covering her with his body, he pushed her face into his shoulder and held his breath, waiting for the next shot.

An eerie hush fell over the canyon, bringing with it a chill that defied the burning rays of the sun. Jessica's heartbeat thundered in her ears, and the acrid taste of fear was bitter on her tongue. Alex shifted to ease his weight from her, and her fingers clutched wildly at his shirt. He'd saved her life. Again. This was getting to be a habit. Hysterical laughter bubbled up in her, the terror that was pulling at her just barely held in check. She'd nearly been squashed by a boulder, and now she'd been shot at. What else could happen?

"Are you hurt?" he asked huskily.

His breath warmly caressed her face as he drew back to stare at her searchingly. Caught between the hard ground and his equally hard body, she found herself trapped in the warmth of his eyes. She dragged in a shuddering breath, and suddenly her tension had nothing to do with terror. His legs were twined with hers, the steel bands of his arms were pressing her to him from chest to thigh, his face was only inches away from hers. Somewhere deep inside her a pulse beat, keeping time with her pounding heart.

She wanted him, she was stunned to realize. Over the last few days she'd tried to convince herself that the sparks of desire she'd felt for him when they'd made that crazy bet had been nothing but her imagination. But this wasn't her imagination. This was the sweetest of aches, something she could barely remember. She watched his lips move, asking her again if she was hurt, but her throat was as dry as the desert, and words were beyond her. She shook her head helplessly.

It always surprised him to see weakness in her. He reached up to wipe the dirt from her cheek, then let his hand linger there, fascinated by the softness of her skin. He should forget what it felt like to have her in his arms, under him, but damn it, she was so easy to touch. And he'd wanted a taste of her for longer than he cared to remember. Just a taste.

Somewhere in the back of his mind, a voice cautioned that he was making a mistake, but he couldn't think of mistakes, not when she was this close. Without a thought, he lowered his head and took her mouth.

Pleasure shot through him at the first touch of his lips to hers, dragging a groan out of him. Oh, God, she wasn't supposed to taste this sweet, this wild. Like wild honey on his tongue. Intoxicating. Delightful. Tempting him to taste all of her—

"Everybody okay?" Charlie suddenly called out. His voice echoed hollowly in the silence. "Jessie? Alex? You all right?"

Alex jerked back as if he'd just been doused with ice water. What the hell was he doing? he wondered wildly, staring down at her wide, shocked eyes and sweetly parted lips. Someone was taking potshots at them, and all he could think of was that she had finally stopped fighting him. The sun must have fried his brains.

He came quickly to his feet. "We're fine, Charlie," he called gruffly to the older man. "Just a little shaken," he continued as he glanced warily at Jessica. "That was too close for comfort."

Shaken? she thought dazedly, fighting back laughter that verged on tears. Shaken didn't begin to describe the emotions churning within her. She could still feel every hard male inch of him against her and the brush of his mustache just before his mouth took hers. He thought they'd been too close for comfort! He was right about that. There was nothing comfortable about the heat he had stirred in her with a kiss that had ended before it began.

"Come on. I'll help you up."

Her gaze flew to his outstretched hand. If she touched him now he'd feel her trembling, but if she didn't he'd know she'd been shaken more by that kiss than she cared to admit. Pride alone wouldn't let her back away.

His fingers had barely closed around hers before she was scrambling to her feet and struggling for a nonchalance she was far from feeling. Forcing a light, careless smile to her lips, she pulled free of his touch and brushed the dust from her clothes. "If throwing me to the ground is your idea of how to treat me like a woman, you're never going to win our bet," she teased huskily, praying he couldn't hear her heart hammering against her ribs.

Alex's gaze narrowed. So she wanted to pretend the kiss had never happened. Maybe it was for the best. He'd known all along that she wasn't the type to enjoy a casual kiss, a casual affair. And he wasn't the type to want anything else, he'd been too long on his own to want strings. If he could just remember that when he touched her, he might be able to get out of the mountains without doing something stupid.

Striving for a lightness to match her own, he acknowledged her criticism with a rueful grin. "Too rough for you, huh? I thought all women liked the caveman type."

Jessica laughed shakily, tension easing out of her. "Being dragged around by your hair isn't all it's cracked up to be." Glancing back over her shoulder to where Charlie and Slim crouched behind several large boulders, their rifles ready, she called out, "Did you guys see where the shots came from?"

"Didn't have time to look," Slim said in disgust.

Charlie shielded his eyes with his hat as he stared at the boxed end of the canyon. "I'd say they came from that cliff. It's a damn good place for an ambush."

It was perfect, in fact. The craggy precipice was at the western end of the canyon, unreachable from the canyon floor. At this time of day, someone could easily hide behind the cliff's rocky outcroppings and pick intruders off like flies in the canyon below. With the sun in their eyes, they'd never even be able to see who their attacker was.

Hovering near the edge of the rocks, Alex waited for the next shot. When it didn't come, he knew their visitor had left as quietly as he'd come. "Think that was our Indian friend trying to scare us off again?" he asked Charlie and Slim as they joined him and Jessica.

Frowning, Charlie pulled a cigar from his pocket and methodically set about lighting it. "Dunno," he said. "Guns ain't usually their way. Course, they might do anything if they're desperate enough."

"It could have been an accident," Jessica said. "Someone could have been target shooting and missed the mark. Or shooting rabbits. It's not un-heard-of, you know."

"You don't look like any rabbit I ever seen," Slim pointed out.

"That's for damn sure," Alex muttered, wondering when he would forget the forbidden taste of Jessica on his tongue. Somehow he knew it would take longer than he cared to speculate. Cursing the Fates, he dragged his thoughts back to the problem at hand. "It was no accident. Stray bullets don't come in pairs. And this is a hell of a place for someone to come for target practice."

Uneasiness slid into Jessica's stomach. "Then if it wasn't the Indians and it wasn't an accident, who was it?"

"I wish I knew," Alex retorted, not liking the suspicions that nagged him as his gaze once again lifted to the cliffs. If someone else had somehow discovered they were digging for three million dollars, they were in a hell of a lot of trouble.

After that, there was never any question that it was time to quit for the day. The camp was as they had left it, already enveloped in the long shadows cast by the low angle of the sun. Charlie took one look at the selection of freeze-dried foods they'd brought along and grimaced. "I think I'll go shoot me a few rabbits for stew for supper. Some real food will taste good for a change."

"I'll go with you," Slim volunteered. "Just in case."

He didn't have to say in case of what. The older man nodded grimly. "Then let's get going so we can get back by dark. No use taking any chances."

"Be careful," Jessica called after them, worry clouding her eyes. Charlie might claim he was hunting rabbits, but she didn't doubt for a minute that he and Slim were going to scout out the surrounding cliffs just to make sure they didn't have any more surprise visitors.

"They'll be okay," Alex told her quietly. For the first time since they'd left her ranch, he and Jessica were alone. If he had any sense, he'd put as much distance as possible between them and escape to his tent until the others returned. He didn't move. "We've probably got at least an hour before they get back. You should get some rest. It's been a rough day."

Her worry vanished in a surprised chuckle. "I can't believe I've got a whole hour to myself. It sounds like heaven." She turned to face him, laughter curving her lips. Her heart did a nosedive as she suddenly realized the camp was empty except for the two of them. She felt her palms grow damp, and stifled the need to wipe them on her dusty jeans. "I . . . I think I'll grab a towel and some clean clothes and go to the springs for a bath. We've been getting back to camp so late in the evenings that I haven't had time." She knew she was chattering, but she couldn't seem to stop. Moving jerkily past the rock where he sat, she said, "If you'll excuse me . . ."

He swallowed a curse and came slowly to his feet. If she insisted on taking a bath, he was going to have to go with her. "I'll go with you," he said flatly. "You're not going off by yourself."

Jessica stopped short and whirled to face him, her blue eyes flashing. The last time anyone had dared to tell her that, she'd been fourteen years old! "And just who died and left you in charge, Mr. Trent?" she asked silkily.

"You almost died, in case you've forgotten," he reminded her roughly. "That bullet came damn close to you this afternoon."

"It's not something I'm likely to forget," she countered. "I'm taking my rifle along, so I'll be perfectly safe. I don't need a baby-sitter."

He'd sworn he wouldn't touch her again, but when she moved past him as if the discussion were closed, his hold on his temper snapped. Without stopping to think, he grabbed her and pulled her back in front of him. "Damn it, for all we know that nut who was taking potshots at you this afternoon is still out there, just waiting for you to go off by yourself. You might be a crack shot, but I don't think that rifle of yours is going to do you a hell of a lot of good when you're buck-naked in the springs, is it?"

Jessica caught her breath in surprise, her heart pounding as her gaze dropped to the fingers gripping her arms before slowly lifting to his face. Anger sizzled in his eyes, burning her with just a look. The Rock of Gibraltar couldn't have been more immovable.

"All right," she sighed resentfully. "Come if you want. But I still don't think it's necessary. I can take care of myself."

He released her, and his dimples flashed outrageously. "But a man can do it better," he teased, and waited for her to explode.

A delicate brow lifted dangerously. "Oh, really? And how is that?"

"He can give her a shoulder to lean on, carry the heavier load, protect her from the world. And love her to distraction in the long hours of the night," he added huskily. At her look of surprise, his eyes locked with hers. "Any more questions?"

She shook her head, afraid to trust her voice, and quickly slipped into her tent. For a long, timeless moment, she stood trembling, fighting back needs she didn't want, wouldn't allow herself to have. Damn him, she wouldn't let him do this to her! She'd learned a long time ago that the only person she could really depend on was herself. She couldn't be tempted into believing otherwise. When they finally came out of these mountains, Alex would go back to Phoenix and she'd be alone. *Again.*

She couldn't afford to forget that, she told herself as she gathered clean clothes, a towel and soap. Her expression was grim. He'd hired her to do a job, nothing more. All she had to do was keep things light and ignore the feelings he stirred in her.

Sure, she thought cynically as she stepped out into the late-afternoon shade and found him waiting. The only problem was that it was hard to ignore a man who had only to smile at you to turn your knees to jelly. Why couldn't he have been fat and bald and pushing sixty?

"Ready?"

"As I'll ever be," she muttered. "Let's go."

They silently made their way to the springs. Jessica determinedly kept her eyes on the rocky ground, her rifle clutched in one hand, her clothes in the other. Alex's long legs matched hers stride for stride. She never slowed her pace, never showed by so much as a flicker of an eyelash that her body was achingly aware of his every movement.

The springs were made up of a series of small streams that bubbled out of the dry ground, the clear, cold liquid pooling among natural basins worn smooth by time. The water gurgled merrily, spilling from one pool into the next before disappearing into the crevices of the mountain as unexpectedly as it appeared. Overhead, three gnarled trees hovered protectively, their concealing limbs dipping nearly to the ground, forming a hidden oasis from all but the most knowing eyes.

But those trees would offer no protection from a man like Alex. Stopping abruptly, she cocked her head, her narrowed eyes shrewd as they met his. "Since you're going to protect me while I'm 'buck-naked,' I presume you're going to stay out here and keep an eye on things."

He grinned wickedly. "Only if you insist."

"I do."

"Somehow I figured you would," he said, laughter dancing in his eyes. "Go on, enjoy your bath. I'm going to sit right here." Easing down against a rock at the edge of the trees, his back to the water, he lifted a dark brow when she hesitated. "Don't worry, I won't peek. You're as safe as if you were in your own bathroom back at the ranch."

Then why didn't she feel safe? she wondered as she slipped under the trees and stared warily through the leaves at Alex. She hadn't felt safe since the moment she'd first laid eyes on him. Whatever the reason, she'd go on struggling, she told herself firmly, reaching for the snaps of her western shirt. There was no room in her life for a man like Alex Trent.

Alex stiffened at the sound of the first snap being unsnapped. Another followed, nearly dragging a groan from him. Damn it, he couldn't see her, but he didn't have to! Unconsciously he counted the snaps in his head and found it all too easy to visualize her fingers traveling down the front of her blouse with agonizing slowness. Her blouse drifted to the ground with a whisper, to be followed by the rasp of her jeans' zipper.

Alex closed his eyes, heat rippling through him to pool in his loins, hot and heavy. Damn it, how was he going to keep his hands off her when she could make him ache without even trying? He should have stayed at camp where he belonged. Maybe she was perfectly capable of taking care of herself—

"Alex? *Alex!* Someone's coming!"

Her low, urgent call sliced through his musing. Without stopping to think, he snatched up his rifle and charged through the trees, his sharp eyes quickly finding her in the water. "Where—"

He stopped dead, stunned. Her hands were buried in lather on top of her head, keeping the soap suds out of her eyes. Her breasts were swaying gently with the motion of the water as it swept past her and disappeared into the rocks. She was magnificent! He could see every inch of her right down to her toes, and from the look in her eyes she was just daring him to comment on it. Desire hit him in the gut like a clenched fist. Desire urged him to forget everything but the need to pull off his clothes and join her in the water.

But someone was coming. He heard it then, the heavy plodding of hooves on the rocky ground, the muttered murmurings of a man talking to himself. Alex's fingers tightened on the rifle. "Sounds like we've got company, all right. Get dressed," he ordered gruffly, and disappeared under the trees to his left.

"Damn!" she groaned softly. She hadn't known it was possible to blush all over, especially when you were sitting in cold spring water. Fighting the fine trembling that started deep in the core of her and spread outward, she quickly rinsed the suds from her hair. Within seconds she was surging out of the water and reaching for her towel with fingers that were far from steady. Would she ever be able to look him in the face again without remembering the desire in his eyes?

Alex took a casual stance by the trees, but every muscle in his body was tensed for action as he watched an old man and his mule slowly make their way toward the springs. The stranger was a stocky man of medium height and indeterminate age. His shaggy brown hair was streaked with gray, as was the ragged beard that concealed the lower half of his face. He wore overalls and a long-sleeved cotton shirt that had obviously survived many washings. On his head was a battered straw hat pulled low over his eyes.

Alex's gaze shifted to the mule, noting the pick and supplies tied to its back. He knew from stories Jessica and Charlie had told that prospectors still roamed the hidden canyons and ravines of the mountains, just as they had for over a hundred years. But they usually distrusted everyone and preferred their own company. They were also usually harmless, but only a fool was taken in by appearances.

If this was the nut who'd taken potshots at Jessica, he was damn well ready for him, Alex thought grimly while cocking his rifle.

The old man froze at the unexpected sound, his eyes watchful beneath the brim of his hat as he looked at Alex standing between him and the springs. His gaze moved from the gun to the hard, unreadable lines of Alex's face. "I just want some water, son," he drawled. "There's no need to pull a gun. I'm unarmed."

Alex studied him thoughtfully, trying to see the face behind the beard and lowered hat. "Can't be too careful up here," he explained, not relaxing his guard.

The prospector nodded, his laughter little more than a wheeze. "You said it there, son. But you ain't got nothing to worry about from me. I just want a little water."

Alex stepped in front of him again, his smile easy, his hazel eyes as sharp as glass. "You'll have to wait a few minutes. My lady's just finishing up a quick bath."

Jessica froze as his announcement carried easily to her through the trees. Irritation made her frown. How easily he claimed her as his! Oh, she knew why he was doing it. A woman alone was always safer when others thought she was under the protection of a lover. But did he have to say it with such ease, as if he really thought of her that way? And did the words have to sound so damn right? She belonged to no man!

Somewhere deep inside her, soft laughter mocked her denial. Who was she trying to convince?

Scowling, Jessica pushed the answer away before it could form. Not today, she told herself. She wasn't ready for it.

Seconds later she was stepping out from under the trees, her hair damp and wild at her shoulders, her yellow camp shirt a bright spot of color in a terrain that was almost colorless but for the trees hanging over the springs. Alex heard her almost immediately and turned. Rational thought scattered under the heat of his gaze.

"All through?" he asked softly.

She nodded. She could, she realized in growing panic, lose herself in his eyes. She deliberately turned her attention to the old man at his side, the smile she forced wavering. Where had she seen him before? "Sorry to keep you waiting," she said quietly. "I wasn't expecting company."

"No problem," the old man chuckled. "You're the first folks me and Bessie seen all day. Bessie don't talk much, so it's kind of nice to run into someone once in a while." Winking slyly at Jessica, he tugged on the mule's bridle. "Come on, Bessie. I know you're as parched as I am."

"You from around here?" Alex asked cautiously, easily keeping pace with him.

He shrugged. "I'm from a lot of different places and no place in particular. Lived all over." At the edge of the trees, he stopped to lift up one of the branches and urge the mule into the shade. "Now if you'll excuse me, I'll get some water. It'll be dark soon and I've still got a ways to go."

He disappeared without a backward glance. Jessica stared after him, then suddenly snapped her fingers. "Now I remember," she told Alex quietly. "I've seen him in town getting supplies. There have been stories circulating about him for years."

"What kind of stories?" Alex asked sharply.

"Oh, the usual kind," she said airily. "He only comes down out of the mountains for supplies, so nobody knows too much about him. There's a rumor he used to be a Wall Street broker who snapped under pressure and came out here to escape from the world. Down at the feed store they say he's a little off and really expects to find the Lost Dutchman." She grinned suddenly, mischief flashing in her eyes. "I guess the same could be said of you."

His own grin was wicked. "Maybe, maybe not." He nodded toward the springs. "Does our friend here have a name?"

"I've only heard him called Dutch. Like I said, he doesn't come down out of the mountains much."

The tree suddenly rustled, and once again the old man and the mule emerged out into the waning sunlight. Wiping his mouth with the back of his hand, he touched the brim of his battered hat in a salute to Jessica and Alex. "Guess I'll be moseying on," he said. "Want to get to Weaver's Needle 'fore the sun goes down."

Jessica watched him disappear slowly among the rocks before glancing at Alex. "Well, what do you think? Is he spry enough to climb up on those cliffs and use us for target practice?"

He shrugged. "Hard to say. He seems harmless, but I'll bet he's as tough as an old boot. Up here, I wouldn't turn my back on him or any other stranger." The grim lines of his face eased a bit as his eyes came back to hers. "Guess I'll take a bath, too. Want to scrub my back?"

"No."

Her answer was short, cool, indignant. Alex grinned and handed her his rifle. "Then I guess you get to keep watch. I'll only be a minute."

"Take two and use soap," she retorted, tossing him hers. "Then I don't have to worry about staying upwind of you."

His eyes glinted dangerously. "You can get right up next to me." He watched the heat climb into her cheeks. "Should be real cozy."

"In your dreams." She sniffed, fighting back laughter. "If you want that bath, you'd better hurry up. It'll be dark soon and we didn't bring a lantern."

"Don't worry, I know where everything is," he chuckled, deliberately misunderstanding her as he slipped under the trees. "If you get nervous, just holler."

"And you'll come running buck-naked," she said, laughing and settling against a rock. "Thanks, but no thanks. I can take care of myself."

His mocking voice floated up to her from under the trees. "I didn't doubt it for a minute. But that doesn't mean someone else can't do it, too."

She bit back a quick retort. Did he think she didn't know what it was like to have a man take care of her? She'd grown up surrounded by men who'd pampered her, spoiled her, watched over her like mother hens sharing one chick.

"I don't need a keeper," she said stiffly as the trees rustled, signaling his return. "I've already got too many—" she began, only to have the rest of her words die on her tongue at the sight of him.

His jeans rode low on his hips, and he wore nothing else but his tennis shoes. Jessica swallowed, unable to stop her eyes from roaming over the lean, hard muscles of his chest, still damp from his bath, to the intimidating breadth of his shoulders, and his dark, wet hair. When he caught her watching him, he grinned, stealing her breath, scattering her pulse. Unconsciously she rubbed her damp palms against her thighs.

"Ready?" he asked.

For what? she wondered wildly, hastily scrambling to her feet before he could offer her a hand up. Something told her that touching him now, when the sun was sinking low in the sky and darkness was starting to seal them off from the rest of the world, would be a mistake. If she ever started, she might not be able to stop.

The thought horrified her.

They left the springs quickly, quietly, tension crackling between them like a hot wire. By the time they reached camp, it was sizzling. One glance at the deserted tents sent Jessica's heart plunging to her knees.

Charlie and Slim weren't back yet.

Achingly aware of their isolation, the ever deepening shadows and the hot touch of Alex's eyes on her, noting her every move, she felt the panic sink into her stomach. She moved to her tent. "I think I'll lie down for a while. Just till Charlie and Slim get back."

She knew from the glint in Alex's eyes that she hadn't fooled him, but she didn't care. She stepped into her tent, only to stop, her hand fluttering to her throat as her eyes widened in horror.

Blood was everywhere—on her clothes, on the tent—its sickly-sweet stench thick on the evening air. There, on her sleeping bag, lay the remains of a dead rat.

Chapter 6

Seeing her fear, Alex crossed to Jessica's side in two quick strides. She stood just inside the open flap with her back to him. He stared at her searchingly, uneasiness twisting in his gut at her frozen stillness. Unconsciously, he reached for her. "Jessica? Are you all right?"

She couldn't move, couldn't seem to drag her eyes away from the nightmare. She swallowed and felt bile rise in her throat. Her fingers moved to her trembling mouth, and in an instant she was covered in a cold sweat. Oh, God, she couldn't be sick! "Alex—"

"Damn it, what is it?" he demanded, turning her to face him. "You're as white as a ghost—"

It was the smell he noticed first, the sickening, cloying scent of fresh blood. Looking past her shoulder, his gaze fell on the dark stains on her clothes scattered about the tent, the mutilated rat lying on her sleeping bag. He swore, a low, biting string of vicious curses, and jerked her to him, burying her face against his chest.

"Let's get out of here, sweetheart," he growled thickly, the endearment slipping out unconsciously as he backed away from the tent with her in his arms. "A little fresh air and you'll feel a lot better. Here," he said, easing her down to the ground near the cold remains of the campfire. Kneeling next to her, he brushed the dark strands of her hair back from her face, his fingers lingering on her clammy skin. He frowned, his hazel eyes dark with concern. "Stay here," he said abruptly. "I'll be right back."

He was gone before she could protest, slipping into his tent and returning a few seconds later with a silver flask. Squatting in front of her, he unscrewed the top and handed the flask to her. "Take a drink. It'll steady your nerves."

At this point, nothing would steady her nerves, but she took the drink anyway. Jessica gasped as it slid into her stomach like liquid fire, chasing away a chill she hadn't even noticed. Tears filled her eyes, but she wasn't sure if they were from the liquor or the remains of terror still lurking in her body. Silently she handed the flask back to Alex.

He watched the color inch back into her face, but she was still pale. Resisting the sudden urge to take her into his arms again, he took a long drink from the flask, then capped it, his expression grim as his eyes locked with hers. "I'm going to check out the rest of the camp to make sure we don't have any more unpleasant surprises," he said quietly, handing Jessica her rifle and reaching for his own. "Shoot anything that even looks suspicious. We'll ask questions later."

He quietly moved through the camp, hardly making a sound as he slipped through the darkening twilight. The tent Charlie and Slim shared was just as they'd left it. Alex had discovered his was untouched when he'd gone to collect the flask. The horses, too, were undisturbed, as was the food and cooking equipment stored near the campfire.

Only Jessica's tent had been vandalized.

As he stepped through her tent flaps again, barely suppressed fury burned in his eyes at the thought of someone sneaking into her tent, violating her things and disdainfully leaving the dead rat where she slept. A muscle rippled along his jaw as his gaze fell on her jeans, blouses and underwear, tossed around haphazardly, splattered with blood. For the first time he noted a vicious rip in the tent from floor to ceiling that could only have been done with a knife. There was violence here, just barely contained.

He wasn't a stranger to violence. Where he'd grown up, it had been a way of life, a spontaneous response to the passion and anger that always seemed to lie just beneath the hot surface of the streets. But there had been nothing spontaneous about this attack. It had been premeditated, malicious, cold. And whoever was responsible had planned it well. Alex didn't doubt for a minute that Jessica had been deliberately singled out for violence. She was the only woman in camp, and therefore the most vulnerable.

His expression was grim as he disposed of the rat. When he rejoined Jessica, he found her pale but calm. At her inquiring look, he said, "It's only in your tent. See anything suspicious?"

"No, but I really didn't expect to." The nausea had finally passed, but the image of the vandalism was still etched in her mind, taunting her. Old fears, old nightmares, still lurked, but she'd be damned if she'd give them the opportunity to terrorize her again. She stood, nervous energy urging her to pace. "I hate to say I told you so," she said quietly. "But I warned you about the Indians. They don't want us here."

"That's too damn bad," he snapped, frustration and worry sharpening his voice. "I'm not leaving." Indians or no Indians, he'd come up here for the money and he wasn't leaving until he got it. But he should never have dragged her into this. Whoever was trying to scare them off was obviously through playing games.

Propping his rifle against a boulder, he turned his back on her and moved to the worktable to light a lantern. "I'll get Charlie to escort you back to the ranch in the morning. I don't want you involved in this anymore. It's getting too ugly."

For a minute, Jessica couldn't believe she'd heard correctly. He wasn't asking her if she wanted to go home. He was telling her! Resentment flared into anger. Who in hell did he think he was? Her blue eyes glinting dangerously, she said flatly, "I'm not going anywhere. You hired me to take you in *and* out of the mountains, and that's exactly what I'm going to do."

"No, you're not, damn it!" he growled, setting the lantern down abruptly. He should have known she'd argue, he thought furiously. "You work for me, and you're going home."

Her chin jerked up. "Who's going to make me?"

Alex told himself later he'd never have touched her if she hadn't lifted her chin and dared him. But, damn her, she knew just what buttons to push to infuriate him. Before either of them had time to blink, he'd eliminated the distance between them in two long strides. He grabbed her, his eyes blazing. "I am, that's who! And if you don't think I can, you just keep pushing me. You've been shot at, nearly killed by a boulder, and now this! What more does it take to convince you you're in danger?"

"I'm in no more danger than the rest of you," she argued hotly. "I wasn't the only one running from those bullets this afternoon. As for the boulder, rocks fall off these mountains all the time. It was an accident."

"And I suppose that dead rat in your tent's an accident, too," he taunted.

He knew he had her there. "That's just another scare tactic of the Indians."

"You're damn right," he agreed, his fingers tightening on her arms to drag her closer. "And it scared the hell out of you and me both. That's why you're getting out of here before anything else happens. Next time, whoever's doing this might not stop at simply scaring you.''

Blue eyes locked challengingly with hazel. "Are we all packing up and leaving, or just me?"

"Just you."

Even before the words were out of his mouth, he could see the fireworks gathering in her eyes. "Send the little lady home when things start to get a little rough, is that it?" she demanded disdainfully, struggling futilely against the hands that held her so effortlessly. "Well, you can forget it! I won't let you or any other man treat me like a helpless female. I'm staying, and there's not a damn thing you can do about it."

"Oh, no?" he growled, snatching her against his chest. "I never said you were helpless, but you're definitely female. And there's not a damn thing *you* can do about that. Maybe it's about time somebody showed you."

"No—"

But it was too late. He took her mouth like a storm sweeping over the mountains, a raging vortex of lightning and thunder, where reason had no place and feelings were everything. Suddenly desire was in her blood, hotter, sweeter, than she remembered. It pulled at her, teasing her, warming her, tempting her to just close her eyes and feel.

And dear God, how she felt! His tongue plundered her mouth, dragging a shudder from her, turning her knees to hot honey. He nipped gently at her lower lip, and the world started to slip from under her feet. Her heart thundered against his, and when his arms crushed her against the long, hard length of him, dark pleasure clouded her mind.

She felt herself sinking, drowning in delight, going under for the third time. Panicking, she struggled against the enchantment, knowing even as she fought for freedom that she was fighting a losing battle.

A distant voice in her head mocked her. Battle? This was no battle; it wasn't even a skirmish. It was a rout, pure and simple, won with a kiss, a touch. She wanted to lose herself in the wonder of it, and only pride made her try to push him away.

In the next instant, he captured her wrists and molded her hips to his. Heat streaked through her like a hot wind off the desert, and she couldn't stop the groan rising in her throat. Without warning she melted, and she couldn't find the strength to care.

Alex pulled her closer and took the kiss deeper, the hunger and frustration that had been building for days twisting in his gut. There *was* passion in her! He could feel it in the barely leashed power of her supple body straining against his, in the throbbing of her pulse at the insides of her wrists, taste it in the hot, moist recesses of her mouth. Her scent swirled around him, surrounding him—soap and spring water and something fresh and feminine and indefinably her. It went to his head like brandy.

His mouth rushed to explore the curve of her cheek, her brow, the pulse pounding in her throat. Need clawed at him. He could, he realized bemusedly, spend days just learning her body with his hands, his mouth, and never come up for air, never need anything but her.

The thought staggered him. He froze, stunned, and stared down at her face, at sapphire eyes filled with desire, at kiss-swollen lips parted in unconscious invitation. It took every ounce of his control not to drag her against him again. Slowly, reluctantly, he released her.

Jessica couldn't have moved if her life had depended on it. Trapped in his turbulent gaze, she tried to think. But how could she, when her thoughts were scattered and her body fairly seethed with emotions that left her weak with longing? Only her battered pride kept her from wilting at his feet.

Damn it, she would not let him do this to her! Sudden anger flared in her eyes. "I don't know what you hoped to gain by that little demonstration, but you wasted your time. All you proved was that you're stronger than I am."

Damned if she wasn't daring him again! Fighting the need to pull her into his arms again, he reached out to caress a dark curl lying just above the curve of her breast. "I proved a hell of a lot more than that, and you know it," he said, a smile flirting around his mouth. "Of course, if you want me to prove it again—"

"No!" The single word was quick, furious, and much too breathless. Before she realized it, she'd taken a step back. "You just keep your hands to yourself."

A sharp whistle suddenly ripped through the growing darkness, cutting off the rest of her words. Charlie stepped into the soft glow of the lantern's light. "Well, I see you two are arguing again. Come to blows yet?"

"You might say that," Jessica said, shooting Alex a quelling glance before turning back to the older man. "Where's Slim?"

"You mean he's not back yet? Damn!" Glaring out at the darkness, which was growing blacker by the moment, he cursed softly. "I followed some animal tracks into a ravine. I told Slim to stay put, but when I got back, he was gone. I figured he must've seen some rabbits and gone after them. Felt sure he'd have returned by now."

"He'll probably show up any minute," Alex said, picking up the lantern with a grim expression. "Right now, we've got an even bigger problem. While you were gone, Jessica and I went to the springs, and we found a little surprise when we got back. Come take a look." He held the light in the open doorway of Jessica's tent.

Charlie's weathered face turned to stone. Under bushy brows, his green eyes were piercing. "Did you see anybody?"

"Only an old prospector," Jessica said from behind him as she quietly laid a fire. "But he came from the opposite direction and was headed for Weaver's Needle."

"We didn't see a damn thing," Alex added as he returned the lantern to the worktable. "Apparently our Indian friends decided to try a stronger warning."

"I don't like it," Charlie muttered. "Somebody's getting real nasty."

Alex's eyes clashed with Jessica's even though he was speaking to the older man. "I want Jessica to go home," he stated, the expression in his face unyielding in the harsh light of the lantern. "But she won't even consider it. Maybe you can talk some sense into her."

"Damn it, Alex, I already told you—" Jessica started.

"Might be the wisest thing to do," Charlie cut in grimly. "We're making someone mighty uncomfortable."

"Then they'll just have to be uncomfortable," she snapped, angry that he was siding with Alex. "Can't you see that we're being manipulated? The Indians obviously think that if they pick on the only woman in the group, the rest of you will give in and get out." Standing, she pitched a last piece of wood on the fire and glared at the two men over the tops of the dancing flames. "Whoever's doing this is a coward who hasn't got the guts to face us. I'm not running from a coward."

Her mind was made up; she wasn't budging. Alex thought she was the most stubborn woman he'd ever met in his life! He turned to Charlie for help, but the older man just shrugged and shook his head. "Don't look at me. When she gets that look on her face, you might as well be talking to one of these rocks. There's no moving her.''

For a tense moment, Jessica and Alex glared at each other like two adversaries squaring off before he muttered a blistering curse and gave in. He didn't know who he was more irritated with, her for being so bullheaded or himself for giving in. ''If one more thing happens,'' he warned her softly, ''you're going home if I have to carry you down out of these mountains myself. And if you don't think I can do it, just try me.''

He'd do it, too, she thought, then quickly banished the image his words brought to mind. But it was hard, especially when she could still feel his hands on her. In growing desperation, she turned to Charlie. ''Did you get a rabbit?''

''Didn't see hide nor hair of one,'' he said in disgust. ''Looks like it's freeze-dried stew for supper. Again.''

It wasn't gourmet fare, but it was edible and filling after a long day of rough work. They sat around the campfire and ate, hardly talking, each lost in their own thoughts. But as they finished and started to clean up, Charlie spoke the worry that was at the back of all their minds.

''Slim should've been back by now.''

''He might have been too far from camp when it got dark,'' Jessica pointed out quietly. It was a flimsy excuse, but the alternatives were unthinkable. ''He knows how dangerous the mountains are at night.

He's probably holed up somewhere waiting for sunrise."

Alex didn't believe it any more than she did, but he didn't argue. "He's got his rifle with him; he should be all right. But if he's not back by the time we finish breakfast, we'll go looking for him."

There was little else they could do. Charlie nodded. "Could be a long day tomorrow. Think I'll turn in."

Jessica's eyes drifted to her tent, and the bloody images she'd carefully relegated to the back of her mind surged forward. The deliberate viciousness of the attack still made her blood run cold, and there was no way she'd be able to close her eyes, let alone sleep, in that tent. But there wasn't another one available. They'd only brought three.

"Take my tent," Alex said quietly, easily reading the emotions chasing themselves across her face. "I'll take Slim's bed for tonight, since he won't be needing it. Tomorrow we'll work out something else."

It was a perfectly logical solution, she told herself. Why then did her heart seem to drop to her knees at the thought of sleeping among his things? Cursing her foolishness, she stood with a casualness she was far from feeling. "That's fine. Guess I'll turn in, too, then." She moved toward his tent, only to hesitate at the entrance. Unable to resist a tug she couldn't begin to explain, she glanced over her shoulder and found his eyes devouring her. Her breath caught in her throat, and before she could do something she knew she'd regret, she slipped into his tent.

Without giving herself time to think, she hurriedly undressed and crawled into his sleeping bag. She knew almost immediately it was a mistake. His scent surrounded her as surely as if his arms enfolded her, a dark, musky fragrance that seemed to seep right through her pores. Memories flared, assaulting her senses. His rakishly wicked smile, his laughter, the soft brush of his mustache before his mouth settled on hers and blocked out thought.

Her pulse throbbed, bringing a sweet ache to the deepest part of her. No! she silently groaned, turning onto her stomach. She wouldn't do this to herself! He'd kissed her, and as much as she hated to admit it, she'd responded. But it was only a physical attraction, she told herself furiously. In all the years since Derrick's death, she'd never let any man get close enough to touch her, let alone kiss her. Of course she'd responded. Any woman with any blood in her veins would have done the same. Alex Trent was a rogue. A wicked charmer with dimples. And he hadn't learned to kiss like that staying at home at night. He'd probably left a string of broken hearts behind him over the years. He could steal a woman's heart before she knew what hit her. She intended to be very, very careful.

Sometime during the night, however, he slipped into her dreams to ridicule her resolve. A phantom lover who laughed at her protests, he kissed her over and over, delighting her senses, awakening her unconscious body with his hands and mouth until she ached with wanting.

She woke with a start, her heart hammering in her chest, her body hot, yearning. It's nothing but a dream, she told herself in disgust, sinking back down into her sleeping bag with a sigh. But she soon discovered it was a dream that had no intention of leaving her in peace. She had only to close her eyes and drift back to sleep to find herself once again tangled in his arms, his mouth on hers.

But the illusion didn't stop. When she woke the last time, he really was there, bending over her, his breath warmly caressing her cheek as he called her name huskily. Her lips tingled. From the kiss he'd given her in her dreams? she wondered dazedly. Or something else?

Suddenly bristling, she eyed him suspiciously. "What do you want?"

She was still tousled with sleep, and she was already spitting at him. Alex grinned, the desire that heated his blood all too familiar. He'd struggled with it most of the night and come to the conclusion that, like it or not, he wasn't going to stop wanting her. Now the question was, what he was going to do about it. "I don't think you're ready to hear what I want," he admitted ruefully, his eyes dancing. "But that's not why I came in here. You overslept. Charlie's just about got breakfast ready."

Startled she gazed at the open tent flap and the weak morning light that spilled in. It was well past dawn. She glanced back at Alex and frowned. He'd changed into clean jeans and a khaki bush shirt, and he looked better than in her dreams. "Just how long were you in here before you woke me?"

"Long enough to change. And you missed it. Too bad." Giving her hair a teasing tug, he stood to leave. "If you want breakfast, you'd better hurry. Looks like we've got a busy day ahead of us."

Something about the way he said the last sentence sent a shiver of apprehension sliding down her back. "Is Slim back yet?"

His smile died. "No."

She swore softly, already reaching for her clothes. "I'll be right out."

A rare morning fog was still clinging to the ragged edges of the mountains when Jessica stepped out of the tent and joined Charlie and Alex around the campfire. Silence, heavier than usual, shrouded the surrounding cliffs in a pearly gray mist that seemed to crawl over the rough terrain. Jessica shivered and wrapped her suddenly cold fingers around the steaming cup of coffee Charlie handed her. She didn't like the fog. It shifted like quicksand, and the ground beneath your feet could vanish into thin air before you had time to scream.

Charlie made powdered eggs and Spam for breakfast, but for once nobody was hungry. Though they tried to ignore it, Slim's absence was an almost physical presence among them. His weathered face tight with tension, Charlie cursed fluently and pushed his plate away. Shoving his hat to the back of his head, he cast a jaundiced eye at the pale, fuzzy orb that was the sun. "This'll burn off soon, and it'll be hotter than hell. Wonder where Slim is."

"He's probably fine," Jessica assured him, and prayed it was true. "You know how easy it is to have an accident in these mountains. One wrong step and you can break an ankle. Don't worry, we'll find him."

An hour later, they left camp on horseback; Slim's riderless horse was tied behind Charlie's. Their canteens were strung over their saddle horns, and their rifles were at the ready. The fog had lifted, and as Charlie had predicted, it was hotter than hell. The very air seemed to singe the lungs. Since they didn't know what direction Slim had taken after Charlie had left him, they decided to search in ever-widening circles around the camp. Spreading out but remaining within view of each other, they began the search.

They searched all day in the heat, every hour taking them farther and farther from camp. They scoured the area where Charlie had last seen Slim, but he wasn't there or anywhere within five miles. So they looked farther afield, worry turning to fear as they lost count of the number of breaks they took, the number of ridges they climbed. He was out there, but where?

When they found him, Jessica wasn't ready. She was urging her mare across a rocky ridge, seeing nothing but dry, barren ground directly in front of her, when a shout from Alex had her hands automatically tightening on the reins. She saw him dismount and disappear into a ravine. Charlie was already there, ready to follow him down into the rocky abyss, when Jessica stumbled to his side.

She clutched at his arm, afraid to look, afraid not to. "Where is he, Charlie? Is he okay?"

The old man shook his head, his face pale beneath a tan it had taken the sun years to bake into his skin. "I don't know. I'm going down—"

But Alex was already coming back up, the muscles in his arms tightening to granite as he pulled himself up the steep incline. When he reached the top, he was panting and his hazel eyes were dark with an emotion that chilled Jessica to the bone.

"He's dead," he said flatly.

Chapter 7

Dead. The words echoed in Jessica's head like a tolling bell out of the past, dredging up visions that had refused to stay buried ever since they'd set foot in the mountains. She shivered, her face as pale as the mist that had shrouded the mountains only hours before. How could she have forgotten how it felt to stand on a cliff and wait for a body to be brought to the top? Helplessness didn't begin to describe the emotions choking her. Anger, denial, a sadness that went beyond tears. And confusion. How could such a thing have happened?

Questions, all they had were unanswered questions! She fumed in frustration as they started the long trek back to camp. Alex had said there was no sign of foul play, but if that was the case, how did a working cowboy with all the grace of an athlete end up at the bottom of a ravine? What had Slim been doing so far from camp when Charlie swore they'd been only a half a mile away when he'd last seen him?

None of it made any sense, but some things never did in the Superstitions.

They arrived back at camp just as dusk was giving way to the darkening shadows of night. Grim, bone-weary, silent, they checked out the tents as carefully as if they were stepping into a mine field. Everything was as they had left it.

She should have been reassured, Jessica told herself. She wasn't. "We need to notify the sheriff," she said quietly, moving to the worktable and the small shortwave radio she'd brought in case of an emergency.

Alex watched her fiddle with the dials, uneasiness gripping him when she frowned and flipped the "on" switch back and forth without results. "What's wrong?" he asked quietly, stepping to her side.

"I don't know." She shrugged, perplexed. "It's dead."

"Maybe it's the battery—"

"No, it's new. I put in a new one before we left the ranch." Swiftly turning the small box around to face the lantern Charlie was lighting, she examined the back, afraid that it had been sabotaged by the same person who'd destroyed her tent. Everything appeared normal. "I don't understand. It was working fine before we left the ranch. I checked myself."

Charlie gave his opinion. "It's these damn mountains," he growled in disgust. "They even do strange things to machinery." His face was hard, unreadable, as his eyes rested on Slim's sheet-covered body which was draped over the back of his horse. "Men wander off by themselves when they got no reason to and turn up dead, and brand new batteries go out without warning. Makes me wonder if the thunder god's put a curse on us after all."

"Slim wasn't killed by any god," Alex said grimly. "And I doubt if he fell off that cliff by accident."

Jessica shot him a sharp look. "Are you saying he was murdered?"

"I'm not saying anything except that we can't rule out all the possibilities."

"Why would anyone want to kill Slim?" Charlie demanded. "He didn't have any enemies that I know of, and I've known him for over ten years."

Alex hesitated. He'd tried to tell himself that all the near misses they'd had since they'd entered the mountains had been nothing but a series of unfortunate coincidences. But he wasn't a man who believed in coincidence, and he couldn't shake the feeling that someone had somehow discovered that he was looking for something a hell of a lot more tangible than the Lost Dutchman. If that was the case, he had to warn Jessica and Charlie about the danger they were in.

Abruptly moving away from the worktable, he searched for a way to tell them and finally admitted, "If Slim was murdered—and I'm not saying he was—

it could have been by someone who's discovered what we're looking for."

Jessica stared at him as if he'd been out in the sun too long. "You can't really believe someone would kill Slim because they thought we were on the verge of finding the Lost Dutchman? That's crazy!"

"We're not looking for that mine," he said quietly. "There's three million dollars in stolen money under those rocks."

The truth was there in his eyes. She gasped and sat down with a thump on the nearest boulder. "Three million—"

"God almighty!" Charlie breathed.

He told them the whole story. Pacing restlessly, he turned to Jessica. "When you assumed I was looking for the lost mine, it seemed safest to let you go on thinking that. I couldn't take a chance then that word would leak out about the money. I'd originally planned to tell you about it once we got up here and started digging, but then you said you'd only agreed to be my guide because you needed the money—"

"So you weren't sure if you could trust me," she finished stiffly, hiding the hurt that tugged at her behind a flash of anger. "Thanks for the vote of confidence!"

"Damn it, Jessica, if I'd have told you at the beginning, you might not have come. I had to get up here. Harlan's dying. I didn't have a hell of a lot of time to waste looking for someone I could trust."

"Trust?" she echoed, seething.

"It was for your own protection," he said in exasperation. "Only Harlan and I knew the whereabouts of the money, and the longer just the two of us knew, the safer you'd be."

"But now you think someone else knows," Charlie cut in, dragging their attention away from each other and back to the danger at hand. "Who?"

Alex sighed heavily. He'd been asking himself that same question ever since they'd found Slim, but with no results. "I don't know. No one except Harlan knows where I am, not even my secretary."

Charlie's gaze drifted back to Slim's body. "I guess we'll never know for sure what happened, but it has to be reported. One of us'll have to go back to the ranch in the morning and notify Jake Sheridan."

It was the only logical solution. And like it or not, Jessica knew that of the three of them, she was the most likely choice. "I'll go," she said quietly. "I know the mountains better than both of you, and you can keep working on the rock slide while I'm gone. It should only take another couple of days to clear it out."

Alex wanted nothing more than to have her out of danger and back at the ranch. But to get there she'd have to wind down the side of the mountain alone, unprotected, easy prey for anyone hiding in the rocks. "No!"

Her back straightened at his tone. "What do you mean, no?" she demanded. "Yesterday you all but threatened to drag me down the mountain yourself if anything else happened. I thought you'd be jumping for joy."

Yesterday he'd had her in his arms, too, and every time he touched her, kissed her, it was harder to let her go. He couldn't take the chance of anything happening to her.

"You can't go alone," he said tightly. "It's too dangerous. And if one of us goes with you, that will only leave one here to dig." And time was slipping away. Turning to Charlie, he said, "Think you can make it back to the ranch by yourself if Jessica gives you directions?"

The older man nodded. "Shouldn't be any problem. I gotta pretty good nose for directions."

"Won't it be just as dangerous for Charlie as it would be for me?" Jessica asked indignantly, her eyes sparkling dangerously.

"Charlie can take care of himself," Alex answered with maddeningly masculine logic. "And," he added, cutting off her gasp of outrage, "he wasn't the one who had a dead rat left in his tent. You've been a target ever since we stepped into these mountains, and if you insist on going back to the ranch, then Charlie's going with you."

The set of his jaw, more than his tone, told her he wasn't going to budge. Exasperated, she stared at him and considered her options. But did she really have any? If she and Charlie went back to the ranch to notify the sheriff, Alex would be left up in the mountains by himself. For reasons she refused to examine too closely, she couldn't leave him, especially since they weren't sure how Slim had died. But if she stayed and let Charlie go instead, she and Alex would be alone together.

Panic and something warmer, sweeter and infinitely more dangerous threatened. She could feel her knees wanting to melt with it and forced herself to stiffen. She had to get out of here, and soon, before she forgot all the reasons she wanted nothing to do with Alex Trent. "All right," she sighed. "I'll stay. But only so we don't lose another week. I want to get out of here as much as you do."

Charlie left just after dawn the next morning with Jessica's clear, precise directions tucked into his shirt pocket, his hat pulled low over his eyes and his rifle ready for the first sign of trouble. Accompanied by the silent burden on Slim's horse, he disappeared from view almost immediately, swallowed up by the mountains.

Jessica stared after him, biting down the words to call him back. She'd spent most of the night telling herself that she was a grown woman and that there was no reason to panic because she found herself alone with a man she was attracted to. All she had to do was throw herself into her work and ignore him.

Hysterical laughter bubbled in her throat. It had seemed so simple in the middle of the night, but there was nothing simple about trying to ignore Alex Trent. He stood at her side, touching her with nothing but his eyes, watching her, waiting. Charlie had only just left, and she was already achingly aware of him. Her heart was racing, and the isolation of the mountains weighed down on her until it seemed as if they were the only two people in the world. Dear Lord, what had possessed her to stay?

Alex watched the emotions cloud the clear depths of her eyes and wondered the same thing. He must have been mad to send Charlie down out of the mountains without her. He could think of a hundred different reasons why he shouldn't want her, but reason didn't have a hell of a lot to do with what he felt when he looked at her. It hadn't from the beginning, and that was what scared the hell out of him. He hadn't lost his head over a woman since he'd been sixteen years old. Now he was dangerously close to losing his heart.

He swung the strap of his canteen around his neck and reached for his rifle. "Let's get to work," he said tightly. "The day's not getting any cooler."

The hours between dawn and sunset were an unending blur of heat, dust, work and tension. With one eye trained on the cliff that surrounded them, Jessica lost count of the number of rocks she moved, the number of times she wiped the sweat from her eyes. Progress was frustratingly slow, and tempers were short. Her arms and back ached, her fingers burned, and when she least expected it she found her gaze slipping to Alex. His shirt was damp from sweat and clinging to his back, his jeans were dirty, and the muscles in his arms rippled as he tossed a twenty-five-pound rock out of the way as if it were no more than a pebble. Her palms went damp just looking at him, and it infuriated her!

Get back to work, she ordered herself angrily. Deliberately turning away, she reached for a rock that weighed fifty pounds if it weighed an ounce. She tugged, swearing as she felt the muscles in her back tighten against the strain.

In the next instant Alex was beside her, his arms brushing against hers, his hands settling only a whisper away from hers on the rough edges of the boulder. "Here, let me help you—"

Something—heat, awareness, desire—rippled from his skin to hers. Jessica gasped and jumped back as if he'd struck her. "I can do it," she snapped. "Don't touch me!"

Did she think he wanted to? he wondered furiously. He couldn't seem to stop himself, and he didn't like it any more than she did! His glittering eyes impaled her. "If I remember correctly, you weren't complaining when I touched you yesterday," he reminded her. "In fact I could have touched you a hell of a lot more than I did."

Heat singed her cheeks. He would remind her of that, she thought resentfully. If she'd been a woman who lied to herself, she'd have flat-out denied his accusation. But she wasn't. "Yesterday was a mistake," she said coolly. "I don't need another man in my life."

"And I'm not looking to be any woman's Prince Charming," he retorted, stung.

"Then you just keep your hands to yourself. Okay?"

"Fine," he said curtly. "That suits me just fine."

"Good. Then let's get back to work."

After that, they didn't speak. Alex left her to the boulder she was so determined to move by herself and deliberately turned his back on her. If he heard her muttered curses, he didn't acknowledge them. Jessica told herself she was glad. If he would just leave her alone, she might get out of the mountains with her heart in tact. Otherwise...

She didn't want to think about what might happen otherwise. It was too dangerous, too tempting, and it was probably far too late to worry about it, she thought hysterically. Dear God, what was she going to do?

She spent the rest of the day doing her best to ignore him and her wayward thoughts. Her mind remained carefully blank of everything but the task at hand. By the time they returned to camp at sunset, she was too tired to do anything but pick at the freeze-dried spaghetti Alex heated over the campfire. Suddenly wanting nothing but to collapse on her sleeping bag, she threw out the remains of her dinner and stood. "I'm going to bed," she told Alex when he looked at her in surprise. It was the first thing she'd said to him in hours.

She disappeared into his tent before he could say a word, taking one of the lanterns with her. Charlie had taken her ruined tent and bloodied clothes back to the ranch. What garments she had left had been moved to Alex's tent that morning. A quick glance assured her that everything was as she had left it, and with a sigh of relief she moved to the soap and water she had set aside for a sponge bath. It didn't compare to a dip in the springs, but it was better than going to bed dirty. Within minutes she'd washed away the grime from the day's work and pulled on a white cotton nightshirt that felt like satin against her clean skin.

When Alex silently stepped into the tent, she was sitting on his sleeping bag, her unbound hair a dark, sensuous cloud on her shoulders as she brushed it with long, languid strokes. The light from the lantern wrapped her in a soft golden glow, turning her sapphire eyes dark and seductive. The delicate lines of her face were breathtakingly lovely and vulnerable. Desire slammed into him, stunning him with its force. He wanted her like that, all soft and feminine and ready for bed. Ready for him. Just looking at her made him ache.

Clamping a lid on the need, he moved forward. Shock widened her eyes when she suddenly spotted him in the doorway. "What the hell do you think you're doing?" she demanded, her gaze narrowing at the sight of the sleeping bag and rifle he carried.

"Getting ready for bed," he said simply, tossing the sleeping bag to the ground so that it rolled out mere inches away from hers. "I'm bushed."

He was serious! She jumped to her feet, the brush still clutched in her hand. "You're out of your mind! You're not sleeping here."

She was barefoot, and the top of her head hardly came to his chin. Alex discovered he liked her that way. "Oh, but I am. For all we know there could be a murderer roaming around out there, and I'm not letting you sleep alone."

"You're not *letting* me—"

"That's right," he said in a tone that brooked no argument. "From now on, we go everywhere together. And I do mean *everywhere*."

The images that flashed before her mind's eye brought a hot flush to her cheeks. "Damn it, Alex, tomorrow you can be my shadow, but you're not sharing this tent with me. Either you go back to Charlie's tent or I will."

"What's the matter? Don't you trust yourself with me in the dark?"

"No!" she gasped, her blue eyes snapping. "It's not me I'm worried about."

"So that's the problem," he said in sudden understanding, his mustache twitching. "You don't trust me."

"Not as far as I can throw you with one hand tied behind my back."

"Ah, Jessica, I'm crushed." With a single step he had her in his arms, one hand wrapped around her slim waist, the other lost in the wild tangle of her hair. Grinning down into her flashing eyes, he felt her breath leave her lungs. He'd only meant to tease her with a touch, a quick kiss, but the tempting feel of her in his arms, covered in nothing but soft, enticing cotton, drove all thought of speed from his mind. This was something to be savored.

"What are you afraid of?" he asked huskily, drawing her closer. "This?" His fingers moved from her hair to the delicate shell of her ear, tracing it with a touch that was as light as the breeze. Every muscle in her body seemed to stiffen in denial, but she couldn't hide the need in her eyes.

"Alex, don't—"

"Or this," he growled, tasting the corner of her mouth, the curve of her cheek, the arch of her brow, before coming back to the sweet nectar of her lips. His mouth settled on hers for the span of a heartbeat, his tongue touching hers, teasing her, withdrawing before she could object, before she could think. "I wouldn't want you to be afraid of this, sweetheart. Never of this."

She wasn't afraid. She was melting like chocolate in the desert sun. She hadn't expected gentleness from him, tenderness. Sweetness. When had she last been given such sweetness by a man? It seeped into her bones, liquifying them, heating her blood until it was hot and heavy and languid. Her eyes closed on a sigh, and her hands clutched at his hard, trim waist. Her knees threatened to buckle. Just a little longer, she promised herself. A taste, a kiss, and then she would remember all the reasons she couldn't let herself want more. "If you're doing this because of that stupid bet—" she began, her voice thick with passion.

"No," he said, stopping her words with his mouth. "I'm doing it because I can't keep my hands off you."

Even as he said it, she surrendered. Alex felt the minute she ceased to think, the minute her body gave in to the desire pulling them both. She dissolved in his arms, slim and subtle and shaped to fit his hands. The ache in his loins deepened to need. With a murmured groan of approval he slipped his hands under her nightshirt to pull her hips to the hardness of his as his mouth swooped down on hers. Her skin, was like smooth, hot satin—almost as soft as the inside of her mouth. He had to touch her. All her secrets, all her heat.

Passion beat at her with silken wings, dragging her down into a swirl of dark needs. His hand moved to her breast, taking her into his palm, his thumb brushing slowly, insistently across her sensitive nipple. She couldn't stop the moan that rose from deep in her throat. Liquid heat coursed through her, dragging pleasure through her veins until she was weak with it.

How could she ever have thought a touch, a kiss, would be enough from this man? she wondered dazedly. She wanted to lose herself in him, to satisfy the hunger that he stirred in her so easily. A night, a week, a month wouldn't be nearly enough.

But in a month, possibly even less, he would be in Phoenix, and she would be back on the ranch, surrounded by a bunch of cowboys whose overprotectiveness would constantly remind her of him.

"No!" she cried, pushing out of his arms.

"Damn it, Jessica—"

"No!" she snapped, backing away. "I don't want this!"

They both knew he could change her mind with one touch. He stared at her in the lantern light, her mouth soft and swollen from his kisses, her eyes dark with desire and something else, something close to panic. It stopped him cold. Her vulnerability always left him helpless.

He turned away and extinguished the lantern, ignoring the fire that burned in his loins. "Go to bed," he said tightly. "I won't touch you again."

She blinked, not sure she trusted him to keep his word. But then his tennis shoes hit the ground one after the other as he tugged them off, and his sigh was heavy on the night air as he stretched out on his sleeping bag. Slowly, hardly daring to breath, Jessica crawled into her own sleeping bag, achingly conscious of his nearness. If she moved an inch, she'd touch him. She didn't move. It was a long time before she slept.

The following day they didn't speak of what had nearly happened, but it became imperative that they get out of the mountains as soon as possible. Desperation kept them working at a frantic pace, ignoring the heat, the thirst that was never slaked, the tiredness that made their arms heavy and their backs sore. What talking they did was carefully limited to their work. They panted and tugged and cursed at the rocks, but they were still achingly aware of each other.

Alex scowled at a boulder that had stubbornly refused to budge despite their best efforts. "I'd kill for a stick of dynamite right now."

"And send the whole side of the mountain down on us?" Jessica retorted, easing the pain in the small of her back with her palm. "There's got to be a better way."

"Yeah. A crowbar," he said in disgust. "Got one?"

"No. I thought the picks would be enough." She sighed, her eyes on the cliffs. "There used to be an old mining shaft stuck in the side of a ravine not too far from here. There might be something there we could use."

He smiled for the first time that day. "Sounds good to me. Come on, let's go."

The mining shaft was where she remembered it, carved out of the side of a ravine less than a mile from camp. To reach it they had to take a narrow path balanced on the edge of the mountain that would have made a goat hesitate. Jessica was glad they'd left the horses at the camp. She wouldn't have trusted that path to anything but her own two feet. Unconsciously she held her breath the entire time they were on the path, and she sighed in relief when they finally reached the safer ground in front of the mine.

Alex cast a critical eye at the rusted metal and old timbers that some unknown prospector had used decades before to dig his way into the bowels of the mountain. The opening was small and dangerous, partially blocked by dirt and rocks. He pulled at a rusty piece of metal, only to see it give way in his hand. "It's all rusted out. And the wood doesn't seem to be much good, either. It's a wonder the shaft didn't cave in years ago."

"Maybe there's something inside that hasn't been so exposed to the weather," she said hopefully, and poked her head into the opening before he could stop her.

"Damn it, woman!" He jerked her back with an arm around her waist. "What are you trying to do? Get yourself killed?"

Her heart dropped to her knees in a dizzy rush at his touch, but she ignored it and gave him a mocking grin. "One of these days you're going to realize I can take care of myself," she told him saucily, holding up a piece of metal that had been half concealed inside the mine entrance. It was rusty but still serviceable. "What do you think? Will it work?"

He didn't give a damn about the metal, not when his body was urging him to turn her in his arms and kiss that smile from her lips. Before the urge could become a need that destroyed reason, he deliberately released her and reached for the metal, testing its strength with his hands. Despite the rust, it was strong. "It just might do," he agreed. "Let's try it out."

They retraced their steps, and Jessica's eyes were on her feet the entire time. Then she felt the first gust of wind. It swept around the sides of the mountain at a fierce pace and nearly pulled her hat from her head. Gasping in surprise, she stopped, grabbed at her hat and looked up at the sky.

Dark, angry clouds swirled around the mountain peaks like a deadly potion in a witch's cauldron. The sun disappeared, and suddenly the very air was heavy, dangerous. Lightning shot down in a sizzling streak of heat and split a huge boulder that stood less than a hundred yards away. The mountains moaned.

With a crash of thunder, the storm was upon them. Before they could gasp, the rain came pouring down in a deluge. Within seconds they were soaked to the skin, the path under their feet as slick as glass, their vision obscured by the rain that beat at them like a hammer.

"Run!" Alex roared.

Jessica tried, but her heart was in her throat and fear seemed to attach lead weights to her feet. Wiping the water from her eyes, she raced after him, but with every passing second he seemed to draw farther and farther away from her.

"Come on!" he called hoarsely when he stopped and saw that she was still far behind. "We've got to get off the side of this mount—"

It happened so fast he never knew what hit him. His feet slipped out from under him on the wet path, and the rest of his words were lost in a broken cry of surprise. The piece of metal they'd retrieved from the mine went flying, and in the next instant he went sliding over the edge of the mountain.

"No!"

Jessica's terrified scream was lost in a roar of thunder that seemed to shake the ground itself. "No, God, no!"

Frozen with fear, she felt an oh-so-familiar horror in her stomach as images of the past flashed before her eyes, threatening to drag her down into the depths of a bottomless nightmare. "No!" she cried, sliding and skidding toward the spot where Alex had fallen. She couldn't give in to the fear, not this time, or she'd be lost.

Gasping for air, for sanity, she threw herself to the ground and clutched at the edge of the path with violently shaking fingers. A sudden spurt of anger pushed the panic aside. "Damn you, Alex, don't you dare die on me, too! I'll never forgive you!"

A chuckle seemed to float on the air just below her. "Then it's a good thing I didn't slide all the way to the bottom of this damn mountain. You'd never let me rest in peace."

"Alex?" Stunned, she impatiently wiped the rain from her eyes and looked frantically over the edge. "Damn it, where are you?"

"Right here, sweetheart," he said. She peeked over the side of the cliff and found him on a ledge fifteen feet below her. "I'm not crazy about the location, but who am I to complain? I'm lucky to have it."

Only a three-foot ledge stood between him and the jagged rocks that waited at the bottom of the ravine. Jessica paled at the thought of what those rocks would have done if the ledge hadn't been there to catch him. "Are you okay?" she asked.

He grimaced at his scraped hands and ignored the cut a rock had made in his side. "Tomorrow I probably won't be able to move, but right now I'm fine. I'd feel a hell of a lot better, though, if I was up there with you."

There was nothing but a smooth expanse of slick, wet rock from the ledge to solid ground. Even if she could reach out to him, Jessica knew she could never pull him up. "I'll have to go back to camp for one of the horses and a rope." She started to leave, then stopped and carefully poked her head back over the side. "I'll be back as soon as I can."

He grinned ruefully. "Take your time. I'm not going anywhere."

The storm beat down all the way back to camp. The stinging pellets of rain lashed at her skin, and the wind whipped her with a violence that took her breath away. Her wet jeans made any kind of speed impossible, but still she hurried on. She skidded over the uneven ground, cursing the bruises she collected from countless falls.

By the time she reached camp, she was covered in mud. Her lungs burned, her sides were heaving. The horses were huddled together, looking miserable in the rain, but she hardly spared them a glance as she headed straight for Charlie's tent and quickly collected the extra rope he'd stored there.

Her thoughts on Alex, she stepped out of the tent again and almost ran full tilt into the grizzled old prospector she and Alex had run into at the springs. She gasped and stepped back quickly, her heart thundering. "Dutch! You startled me. Wh-what are you doing here?"

"Bessie and me was on our way to the caves east of here when this dang storm blew up out of nowhere," he said, adjusting the set of his hat when rain ran off its back brim and dribbled under the collar of his poncho. "Just wanted to make sure you and that man of yours were all right. You know, it's awfully isolated up here. A body could get in a heap of trouble before he knew it and have no one to turn to."

A shiver slid down Jessica's back at his words. Oh, yes, she knew all about the different kinds of trouble you could get into in the Superstitions, but she didn't have time to discuss them with this lonely old man. "We're just fine," she assured him. "If we get into any trouble, we've always got our rifles. Now if you don't mind, I'm in a hurry. Alex is waiting for me."

"Sure, sure," he said gruffly. "Well, I guess me and Bessie'll head for the caves, then."

He moved off in a slow, ambling gait that defied the rain. Frowning in confusion, Jessica watched him until he disappeared into the downpour. What a strange old man, she thought, and hurried to her mare.

Chapter 8

With each moment she was away from Alex, the storm grew fiercer, angrier, until the mountains seemed to moan and weep with pain. Jessica wondered if she'd descended into the fires of hell. The rain came down in sheets, wrapping the dangerous terrain in a cloak of gray mist that changed the shape of landmarks and made even the familiar strange. At times, instinct alone guided Jessica. The wind beat at her, sweeping her hat from her head and throwing her wet, tangled hair into her face until she could hardly see. Dragging the dark strands out of her eyes, she cursed when the mare suddenly shied at the thunder that cracked directly overhead. Memories now etched in the back of her mind demanded entrance to her thoughts, but her fingers only tightened on the reins, and determination hardened the set of her jaw. No, she told herself furiously as she urged the mare up a rocky ridge. She wouldn't let the past haunt her now. Later she would somehow find a way to cope with the déjà vu sickening her, but right now she couldn't afford the pain.

Her nerves were knotted with tension by the time she reached the cliff trail again. In the short time she'd been gone, the trail had also changed. The rain had already eroded the path until it seemed to teeter on the very edge of the cliff. Apprehension dropped into her stomach just at its sight. It looked as if it were ready to slide right off the face of the mountain.

If that happened, Alex would go with it.

The thought slipped in before she could stop it, horrifying her. She blanched. Her fingers shook as she quickly dismounted and tied one end of the rope she'd brought to the saddle horn. "Alex?" she called hoarsely, suddenly afraid only the mountains would answer her call. "Are you all right?"

"Oh, yeah," he retorted. "I'm on top of the world. *Get me out of here!*"

At any other time, Jessica would have laughed at his roar of frustration, but she couldn't allow herself to relax until she got him off that ledge. "Hang on. I'm coming."

Cautiously making her way toward the spot where he'd fallen, she dropped to her stomach and tried not to notice the way the ground disappeared into nothingness just inches away from her face. She tensed, her fingers curling in the mud, and eased forward until her head extended over the edge of the cliff. She could see him, but her heart jumped into her throat when she did. He was flattened against the sheer cliff wall in order not to be snatched from the ledge by the wild rush of the wind.

"I'm going to lower the rope to you," she told him with a calmness she was far from feeling. She nudged it over the side. "Wait!" she cried. He'd reached for it just as the wind had started up, making the rope swing crazily. "I—I'll pull it back to you."

He caught it on the third try and had it tied around his waist before Jessica's sigh of relief had died on the wind. After giving it a last jerk to make sure it would hold, he looked up. "I'm ready when you are. Let's take it slow and easy."

She nodded. "Just hang on tight and let the mare do the work. She'll have you up in no time."

In five minutes he was crawling over the side of the cliff. His dark hair was plastered to his head, and his face and arms were scraped and bleeding. Mud covered him from head to foot. Jessica was unable to stop trembling now that the crisis was past. He was wet, dirty, wonderful. She wanted to laugh, to cry, to run to him and catch him in her arms. Instead she stood, unable to move, unable to think of anything except that she'd almost lost him. When had he come to mean so much to her?

For what seemed like an eternity he lay in the rain and mud, his chest heaving, sending up a silent prayer of thanks. Solid ground. If it hadn't been so muddy he'd have kissed it. Laughter pushed aside the tension still knotting his muscles. He glanced up to tell Jessica that he must look as if he'd been rolling in a pigsty. Then he caught sight of her face. Her skin was as pale as death, her dark blue eyes wide, stricken. She was leaning against the mare as if she'd collapse without its support.

Concerned, he jumped up and started for her, unmindful of the rope still trailing around his waist. "Jessica? What is it?" he asked, reaching for her.

His fingers settled on her shoulder with a gentleness that brought the sting of tears to her eyes. Horrified, she quickly blinked them back and clutched at the tattered shreds of her pride. She would not fall apart over this man! "I—I'm fine," she said huskily. "We should get back to camp. It'll be dark soon with this storm."

Puzzled, he searched her eyes, a frown darkening his brow as he watched her. "I'm fine, you know," he said softly, his fingers tightening reassuringly on her shoulder. "Thanks to you. No telling how long I would have been stuck on that cliff if it hadn't been for you."

Don't be kind, she thought desperately. Not now. She just couldn't handle it. "Don't thank me. If I hadn't brought you up here, you'd have never ended up on that ledge." Turning her back on him, she untied the rope from around her saddle horn. "I'm sorry I didn't bring another horse, but I didn't want to take the time."

"No problem. We'll ride double." Before she realized his intentions, he swung her up in the saddle, coiled the rope and handed it to her, then stepped into the stirrup and came up behind her.

His arms surrounded her, pulling her back against the solid wall of his chest, stealing her breath and making her achingly aware of his hard thighs caressing hers with every step the mare took. Heat licked at her senses, destroying the protests that struggled to form on her tongue. They rode back to camp in a silence as thick and explosive as the thunderstorms that enveloped the mountains.

The camp was wet and gloomy in the growing darkness. The tents were just barely braced against the fiercely blowing rain. Alex swore in disgust. "Damn this storm! It's going to blow us right out of here if we're not careful." Quickly dismounting, he handed her the reins. "I'm going to tighten down those guy lines before the tents collapse and we have to spend the night in the rain. You take care of the mare and check the other horses."

The wind howled like a banshee, making their work twice as difficult. Jessica hurriedly unsaddled the mare, then moved to help Alex when she saw Charlie's tent wobble precariously. They secured it, then checked the others. Only then were they able to escape into the tent they were sharing and to pull the flap down, closing out the storm.

And closing them in.

Jessica felt her heartbeat quicken and told herself not to be a fool. She lit the lantern and turned to face Alex, frowning at his scraped face as she would at one of her sons. "I need to clean those scrapes," she said in a no-nonsense voice. "You don't want to get an infection."

He spread his arms. "I'm all yours."

His husky words stroked her like velvet. She shivered, unconsciously stepping back until the top of her head brushed the pitched ceiling of the tent. In the next instant, she gasped as he pulled her back in front of him. Laughter danced in his eyes, but he only said, "Don't touch the tent. It'll leak."

If there had been a hole close at hand, she'd have crawled into it. Fire singed her cheeks, and in growing desperation she whirled to search for the first aid kit. She found it almost immediately and clutched it to her like a shield as she turned to face him again. "If you'll take your shirt off, I'll put some antiseptic on those cuts."

Alex couldn't remember the last time a woman had fussed over him. His mother hadn't had much patience with a rough-and-tumble son who was always falling from one scrape into another, so he'd soon learned to take care of himself. The world he'd grown up in had bred toughness and mocked any sign of softness. Over the years, he hadn't encouraged the women in his life to soothe his aches and pains.

But he liked the idea of Jessica's hands on him. His fingers went to the buttons of his shirt, and his smile was slow and sexy as his eyes locked with hers. "Be gentle with me," he said huskily. "I have a low pain threshold."

Jessica opened her mouth to come back with a smart retort, but when he shrugged out of his shirt and let it slide to the ground, she couldn't remember what she'd been about to say. The tent suddenly seemed too small, Alex too close, too big. The soft light of the lantern traced the strong lines of his chest with loving fingers, running over the hard, lean muscles, the broad shoulders, the firm waist and the trim hips molded by his wet jeans. Water clung to his bronzed skin, catching the lantern light, drawing Jessica's eyes like a suncatcher. She wanted to touch him, to explore every inch of him. Her fingers fairly ached with the need.

Wild color flooded her cheeks, and her chin came up with a snap. Damn it, she wouldn't drool over him like a sex-starved widow! Stepping purposefully toward him, she jerked open the first aid kit and pulled out the antiseptic. "This could sting a little," she warned, soaking a piece of cotton in the liquid, then quickly dabbing it on the lacerations on his face and chest.

He flinched. "Hey, that burns!"

It couldn't burn nearly as much as the flames that sparked to life deep inside her at the feel of his skin under her hands. She could feel the heat all the way to her toes. Dragging in a shuddering breath, she desperately tried to examine his injuries with clinical detachment. But how could she when her fingers looked so small and delicate against his shoulders and the granite hardness of his jaw? She swallowed. "Don't be a baby," she said huskily. "It'll only sting for a minute."

His hands settled at her waist, and he looked into her eyes. Her fingers stilled at his jaw. "Are you going to kiss it and make it better?"

"No!" she cried, too quickly. He was coming to mean too much to her. If she kissed him now, she'd give him more than a kiss, more than her body. He'd have her heart and soul, and when they left the mountains she'd lose him. She knew what it was like to lose a man. She'd couldn't stand the pain a second time.

Jerking free of his touch, she replaced the antiseptic in the first aid kit and turned to put it with the personal items she kept at the foot of her sleeping bag. Alex caught the haunted look in her eyes. He frowned. She was still too pale, and he'd felt her trembling all the way back from the cliff. He wanted to take her in his arms and comfort her, but she kept turning away from him, making it clear she didn't want his touch. And he wanted to do a hell of a lot more than touch her! She was driving him crazy.

"You need to get out of those clothes," she said tightly. "You're soaked."

"So are you."

"Do you want to go change first, or shall I?"

Amusement slid into his eyes, pushing concern aside. "Oh, you can. I'm in no hurry."

Something in his tone sent her heart pounding. She whirled, as wary as a cornered cat. "If you think I'm going to undress in front of you—"

"It's either that or sleep in wet clothes, because I'm not leaving this tent again tonight and neither are you.

It's still pouring out there." He watched her eyes flare at that and grinned. He much preferred it to the haunted look he'd seen there earlier. "You don't have to be ashamed of your body, sweetheart," he teased outrageously. "I've seen you without your clothes. You're beautiful."

He would remind her of that! Cursing the heat that flooded her cheeks, she met his eyes unflinchingly. "I'm not changing in front of you."

Alex's grin broadened. Damn, she was stubborn! And far too tempting with her wet clothes clinging to every delectable curve of her body. If she didn't change—and damn quick—he wasn't going to be responsible for his actions. Turning his back on her abruptly, he said, "You got five minutes. Take it or leave it."

Jessica stared at his naked back and knew this was the only concession he was going to make. She quickly tugged off her wet sneakers, then her jeans, cringing at the rasp of the zipper. She unconsciously held her breath as her fingers soundlessly slipped the buttons of her blouse free, and her eyes never left Alex's broad shoulders. Her heart thundered as she dropped the blouse and then her wet bra, the snap of its clasp like a rifle shot in the tense silence that filled the tent. He stiffened, and her heart jumped into her throat as she reached for her nightshirt.

Cursing her own skittishness, she searched for something that would break the tense silence. Suddenly she remembered the old prospector. "When I came back for the mare, I ran into Dutch."

"What!" Cursing, he spun to face her, catching her with her nightshirt half-on, her creamy skin golden in the lantern's light. Desire punched him in the stomach, and it took all his control to ignore it. "Where? What happened?" he demanded.

Hot color burned her cheeks as she yanked her nightshirt down and resisted the urge to defensively cross her arms over her breasts. "He...he was just coming into camp when I stepped out of Charlie's tent," she explained. "He said he was afraid something might have happened to us in the storm so he thought he'd better check on us." At Alex's snort of disbelief, she frowned. "You think he was up to something?"

"Damned if I know," he said tightly, desperately trying to ignore the way her nightshirt clung to every sensuous curve. "What kind of nut goes out in an electrical storm to check on two people he hardly knows?"

How could she talk about Dutch when the stroke of his eyes almost melted her bones? Jessica wondered wildly. Her fingers curled into her palms. "He claimed he was on his way to the caves east of here when the storm hit. He knows how isolated we are and wanted to make sure we weren't in any kind of trouble."

The only trouble Alex was worried about right now was the kind he would be courting if he took the single step that would bring Jessica into his arms. "We're isolated, all right," he muttered. "I'll be damn glad when Charlie gets back."

Jessica silently seconded the thought. Every day they were alone together, every night he spent within inches of her, he came closer and closer to stealing her heart.

Suddenly weary, she sighed and dropped to her sleeping bag. "I don't know if Dutch was up to something or not, but I can't worry about it any more tonight. It's been a long day. I'm going to bed." Without another word, she crawled into the sleeping bag and turned her back on him.

Alex stared at her in disbelief. The throbbing of his body reminded him they were miles from anywhere, trapped in the tent by the rain. Whether Jessica wanted to admit it or not, they wanted each other. The air was thick with it. How could she sleep when they both knew it would only take a touch to bring her into his arms? Was she really so cool? She made him feel like a raw teenager who hadn't learned to control his hormones.

It was infuriating! he thought in disgust. He turned out the lantern with a vicious twist. Stripping out of his wet clothes and shoes, he slid into his sleeping bag, determinedly ignoring the desire clawing at him with hot fingers.

Lightning ripped the sky open without warning, and the rain came down in torrents. Within seconds it had collected in the mountain canyons like a raging river, sweeping everything from its path in a wild rush to the desert floor below. Crying out in alarm, Jessica grabbed madly for the rocks that cut into the side of the cliff. Fear choked her and made her fingers stiff as she climbed painfully up the side of the cliff. Behind her, Derrick's breath was ragged and hoarse as he followed, pulling himself free of the dangerous drag of the water. Jessica wanted to turn around and tell him they were almost at the top, but she didn't have the breath. Gasping, she felt for the last foothold and sent herself rolling over the top. Hysterical laughter bubbled in her. They'd made it!

"Jessica!"

The horrified call caught her in the middle of a laugh. She jerked up in alarm and saw Derrick's fingers slipping on the rocky edge, his terrified eyes pleading with her to help. With a startled cry she clutched at him, but his weight was too much. Slowly, inexorably, he was torn from her grasp. She whimpered, grabbing for him, and watched in stunned surprise as he somehow turned into Alex before her very eyes. In the next instant his fingers were jerked from hers, and his scream of terror echoed in her ears as he dropped away from her into nothingness.

"No!"

She sat bolt upright, horrified, her breath tearing at her lungs, and stared wildly at the shadowy confines of the tent. A dream, she realized dazedly, shuddering as her eyes found the dark outline of Alex sleeping only inches away from her. It was only a dream. Tears stung her eyes, her throat, choking her. With a muffled cry, she buried her hot face in her shaking hands.

Alex woke to the sound of her almost soundless sobbing. He sat up in alarm, reaching for her before he was even fully awake. "Jessica? Sweetheart, what is it?"

"N-nothing. I—I'm s-sorry..."

His arms closed around her in the darkness, pulling her against his chest, his fingers tangling in her hair to bury her face against his throat. He'd seen her frightened, spitting mad, stubborn and indignant, but never like this. Never helpless. His arms tightened around her. "Tell me," he said, pressing a kiss to the top of her head. "What happened? Did you have a bad dream?"

"My h-husband—" She clutched at him, swallowing a sob. "He died up here s-six months after we were married." Her defenses down, she blurted out the past in jerky sentences, telling him how she hadn't been strong enough to stop him from falling to his death, how she'd blamed herself and had just wanted to die. On her nineteenth birthday, she'd learned she was pregnant. And then the boys had been born, and she was the only one they had to depend on. Sometimes it was so hard being the strong one.

Stunned, Alex pulled her closer. She'd been little more than a child when she'd had three babies at once, all without the love and support of her husband. Tenderness welled up in him, surprising him with its strength. He was a considerate lover, but he'd never allowed himself to feel the sweeter emotions with a woman. But this woman he wanted to protect, to cherish.

Murmuring reassuringly, he kissed the tears from her eyes, the gentle curve of her cheeks, the corner of her mouth, wanting only to comfort her. But somewhere between her cheek and her trembling lips, he got lost in the taste of her. She tasted of the night, dark and intoxicating, and was soft with the lingering traces of sleep, warm. A sweet, aching pleasure seeped through him, and he sighed as his mouth settled over hers.

He felt the moment the painful memories left her. She stilled, and a soft gasp of surprise touched his lips. Her hesitation twisted his heart. He wanted to crush her against him, to drive everything out of her mind but the taste and feel of him loving her. But he couldn't push her, not when there were still tears on her cheeks and she seemed so delicate and breakable in his arms. His hands came up to capture her face and pull her gently away. His gaze found hers in the darkness. "Jess?"

The choice was hers. She could hear it in his voice, feel it in the sudden stiffness of his body. One word from her and he'd let her go. Another time, another night, she might have said it. But not tonight. Not when she could still see his face when he'd slipped from her grasp in that dream. "Love me, Alex," she pleaded, leaning forward to kiss him sweetly. "Please."

His breath rushed out in a sigh of relief. "Come here, sweetheart," he growled, and swept her out of her sleeping bag and into his before she had time to do anything but gasp as his naked body slid along hers.

He didn't have to ask how long it had been since she'd been with a man. He didn't doubt for a minute that it had been years. So much passion, love, heat locked away, he marveled, resisting the urge to rush. He wanted to make it all up to her, to slowly peel away layer after layer of her restraint until she came undone in his arms. And he'd start with her mouth. It had always fascinated him.

He pressed the lightest of kisses to her lips, nibbling at her, his tongue tracing the sensuous outline before dipping inside to taste, to linger, to stroke. A shudder rippled through her, and she reached for him blindly as the ground seemed to shift beneath her. It had been so long. . . .

Had she forgotten what it was like to have a man's hands on her, making her ache with need? Or was this something new, different, sweeter? He touched her thighs in a lazy caress, and she forgot to breathe. When his hand slid under her nightshirt and moved with painstaking slowness to her breasts, she forgot to think. And when his mouth traveled to her ear, to the pulse pounding in her throat, to the rosy crest of her breast, she floated. Her fingers clutched at him, sliding into his hair to cup his head to her breast, her breath fast and shallow as his tongue flicked out to caress her, wetting her nightshirt. Lightning streaked through her, leaving traces of heat in her blood. "Alex—"

"I know, sweetheart," he groaned, struggling to find his breath. "Let's get you out of this nightshirt. I want you against me. All of you."

In the blink of an eye she was as naked as he, his hair-roughened legs entwined with hers, his arms crushing her to his hardness, her heart slamming against his. Dark needs pulled at her, and with a murmur of pleasure she moved against him. Her own hands moved down his back, to his waist and to the strong muscles of his shoulders and chest. She explored him hesitantly, uncertainly, with a touch that was as light as a feather.

Alex caught his breath, the pleasure that pulled at him bordering on pain as her hands moved lower, past his waist, only to stop. He'd never expected shyness from her. His fingers caught hers and dragged her hand down to where his body was on fire for her touch. "Touch me, sweetheart," he said thickly.

That was all the encouragement she needed. His breath hissed through his teeth as her fingers closed around him, caressing him lovingly, driving him to the brink of madness. It was torture of the sweetest kind, turning him inside out, inflaming him. He stood it for as long as he could, but he'd never been quite so susceptible to a woman's touch before. His control started to unravel with a speed that stunned him.

"Enough," he groaned, pulling her hands from him. His heart raced against hers, and his eyes found hers in the darkness. They were heavy with desire, cloudy with need. His fingers laced with hers. He'd dreamed of her like this. All hot and soft beneath him, weak with longing. He'd wanted her longer than he could remember, and now she was his. With a muffled groan, he swooped down to take her mouth at the same time he slipped into her silken heat.

Jessica felt something inside her soften and give way to delight and a pleasure so intense it brought tears to her eyes. He moved slowly, stroking her, and excitement ripped through her, pushing her closer to the edge. Desire swirled in her blood, pulling at her until she nearly cried out with the joy of it. Somewhere in the distance thunder echoed, and suddenly the pounding was inside her, tugging her to the edge of nothingness. Her fingers tightened around his. "Alex!"

Her startled cry snapped the last remnants of his control. "Go with it, sweetheart," he growled hoarsely. "I've got you." And with a single stroke he sent them both into a dark, raging storm of lightning and thunder.

He woke at dawn, the sleepiness that fogged his brain vanishing at the feel of the woman in his arms. She slept against him as if she had done so for years. She used his shoulder as a pillow. Her breasts were soft and enticing against his chest, and her bent knee was casually thrown across his thigh. Heat stirred in him, urging him to wake her slowly with his mouth, his tongue.

But even as his arms started to tighten around her, he was thinking of the night. She'd dreamed of her husband, cried for him. While he'd loved her long into the night, had she been thinking of another man?

Biting back a bitter oath, he released her and silently eased out of the sleeping bag. Grabbing underwear, jeans, a black T-shirt and his shoes, he stepped outside to dress, all the while cursing the mountains. Too late, he realized he hadn't been thinking clearly ever since he'd urged his horse up that first ridge. He had no business wanting a woman like her, but he did, damn it! He ached for her, and he couldn't even be sure she wasn't still mourning her dead husband!

He wasn't going to touch her again until they were back in the real world, he decided. The lines of his face were grim. When they were both thinking clearly, he'd see if what they shared was something more than a stolen night in the mountains.

When Jessica found him an hour later he was already hard at work, hammering away at the boulder they hadn't been able to move yesterday with the pick, turning the air blue with his curses. He was drenched with sweat. His black T-shirt clung to the rippling muscles of his back.

She hovered uncertainly behind him, not sure how to greet him. She had no experience with morning-afters. Had last night been as wonderful as she remembered, or had her dreams colored it with fantasy? That morning, she'd reached for him in that timeless moment between sleep and wakefulness and touched only the coolness of the sleeping bag. She hadn't even felt him leave. Why did that make her want to cry?

Resisting the need to hug herself, she straightened her shoulders, her expression carefully blank as she advanced toward him. "Good morning."

His gaze swung to hers, and his jaw clenched. She wore a simple cotton blouse and the inevitable jeans. Her sable hair was pulled back in a ponytail that made her look about sixteen. But no sixteen-year-old could make him ache like she did, he reminded himself as his gaze roved over her hungrily. There was something different about her today. She was softer, more vulnerable. Had his loving changed her so much?

Scowling at the thought, he growled, "Good morning," and turned his attention back to the rock he'd been beating for the last hour. Glaring at it, he swung the pick in a mighty arc and shattered the boulder with one swing.

Hurt pierced her heart as surely as if one of the shards of rock had struck her. What had she expected? she wondered. That he'd sweep her into his arms and carry her back to the tent? If he'd wanted her this morning, he'd never have left her.

He wouldn't have another chance to leave her, she vowed. Last night had been a mistake, one she didn't intend to repeat. She'd stupidly allowed herself to forget who he was, who she was. Their time together had limits, and at the end of it he'd leave without a backward glance. She couldn't afford to forget that.

Stopping to wipe his brow with his forearm, Alex spared her a brief glance before determinedly looking back at the pile of rocks. "If we keep a steady pace, we might be able to clear the rest of this today. I don't know about you, but I'm ready to finish up and get out of here.

She winced, but he didn't see it. Obviously, last night had meant nothing to him. How stupid of her to think that it would. "Fine. I can't wait to get back to the ranch."

After that, they didn't talk much. Sometime during the long day of digging, the hostility that had sparked between them from the day they'd met disappeared, leaving in its stead an intimate sense of awareness that drew them together despite their best efforts to remain indifferent. They tried to ignore each other, but that awareness was always there, making each of them conscious of the other's slightest movement.

By the middle of the afternoon, the strain of pretending that nothing had changed was more than Jessica could bear. Images of the previous night kept taunting her until she wanted nothing more than to walk into Alex's arms. The idea horrified her. She couldn't let herself need his strength, his touch, his loving. What would she do when he left?

Alex watched the emotions skitter across her face and just barely fought back the urge to reach for her. It was an urge he'd been fighting all day. He couldn't make the mistake of touching her again. Not until they got out of the mountains.

Scowling, he tossed a rock out of the way, his back muscles straining from the weight. Then he turned back to lift another, but there was nothing there but a small opening that seemed to lead into the side of the mountain.

The cave!

Alex let out a whoop of excitement and grabbed Jessica and whirled her around before either of them had time to think. "This is it, sweetheart! The cave! I knew we'd find it!"

Jessica clutched at him, laughing in surprise, her head spinning. "What cave? Alex, put me down. I can't think."

"You don't need to," he said, laughing. "We've found the money. This is where Harlan hid it. Can you believe it? It's been hidden for thirteen years and we're the first to find it!" Releasing her, he turned back to the cave opening, which was still partially blocked by rocks. "C'mon, help me clear out the rest of this."

Catching his excitement, she moved to help, and in less than thirty minutes they had the cave opening cleared. The cave was small, barely six feet in height and little more than that in width. It reached back into the mountain about twenty feet before taking a sharp turn to the left, where it grew narrower, darker.

Using one of the lanterns he'd retrieved from the camp, Alex had to stoop as he took the lead and stepped into the blackness. Her heart in her throat, Jessica followed close behind and prayed the cave was as sturdy as it looked.

They came to its end before she was ready, and she bumped into Alex's back before she realized he'd stopped. When she looked past him and saw the pile of rocks that cut off further progress, her hands turned clammy. "A cave-in," she whispered, her voice echoing eerily in the heavy silence that engulfed them.

"No, it's been dynamited," Alex said quietly, setting down the lantern. "Harlan's a dynamite expert. The money's just on the other side of these rocks. Stand back," he ordered hoisting the pick he'd brought. "I'm going to clear it away."

In the thirteen years since Harlan had dynamited the cave, the rubble concealing the money had shifted and settled until it was almost as immovable as the mountains themselves. Alex cursed and sweated and pounded at the rocks, but in the end he was only able to carve out a small tunnel that opened onto the other side. Cursing, he blinked against the sweat that stung his eyes, and glared at the rocks. "Damn! It'll take days to dig it out enough so I can get through without getting stuck."

"I can get through it now," Jessica said, measuring it speculatively. It was small, but she should just be able to squeeze through. Jumping up from the rock she'd been sitting on while he'd worked, she dusted off her jeans and came forward eagerly. "I'll just slip through to the other side and hand the money back to you."

"No!"

Jessica stiffened, her eyes flashing dangerously at his autocratic tone. "I don't need your permission," she reminded him softly, too softly.

Even in the stark light of the lantern, he could see the dare in her eyes. He swore, curling his fingers into his palms to keep from reaching out to shake her. "We don't know what kind of damage the dynamite did on the other side," he said angrily, trying to reason with her. "If you got into some kind of trouble over there, there would be no way I could get to you. It would take me days to dig my way to you."

"I'll be careful."

"I was careful on that cliff yesterday and look what happened."

"Damn it, Alex, I'm not made of spun glass. I don't break that easily."

No, she didn't break. She was strong, independent, self-reliant, beautiful. From the very beginning he'd fought the attraction that pulled him to her. He hadn't planned on falling in love with her, but something deep inside him told him he wasn't going to be able to avoid loving Jessica Rawlins. It was already too late.

The sooner he got out of the mountains, the better. "All right." He sighed. "But take the lantern with you and make sure it's safe before you step through to the other side."

She didn't give him time to change his mind. Carefully holding the lantern in front of her as she wiggled through the tunnel, she fought down rising panic as the rock seemed to close around her. It wasn't far, she told herself determinedly. Then she gasped as her head and shoulders suddenly cleared the tunnel.

This part of the cave was even smaller than the section where Alex waited. Impossibly it was also darker, and the air was stale. The lantern light glistened off the black rock walls and ceiling. Jessica searched for weaknesses, but it looked as strong as a brick house. She sighed in relief. "It's all right, Alex," she called back, her words echoing hollowly. "It's safe."

The last of the light disappeared with her, leaving Alex to worry in the dark. If something happened to her, he'd never forgive himself. "Check the left side," he said. "Harlan said there was a pocket in the rock there near the floor. He stuck the money in there. It's in a metal case."

Jessica squatted down and saw it almost immediately, the gleam of metal in the lantern light. She reached for it with shaking fingers. "My God, Alex, it's here! I don't believe it!"

Triumph flashed through him like quicksilver. It was there, damn it! After thirteen years! Closing his eyes, he laughed in delight. "Good girl! Hand it through the tunnel to me and then get over here. I want to kiss you!"

The money came through first, then the lantern. Then Jessica. Alex took one glance at her grinning face as she poked her head through and grabbed her, dragging her free and into his arms for a fierce hug and a kiss that turned her knees to water. When he finally lifted his head, they were both breathless and laughing. "Hot damn, lady, we did it! Let's get out of this hole and celebrate."

Snatching up the metal case as if it weighed no more than a few pounds, he handed her the lantern. Then he slipped his other arm around her shoulders. Within minutes they were at the cave's entrance, standing in the sunlight, grinning into each other's eyes.

Alex moved his hand from her shoulder to her cheek, lazily rubbing at the streak of dirt there. "You need a bath, lady," he growled softly.

"You could use one yourself," she countered, chuckling. "If you'll scrub my ba—"

Without warning, the sharp crack of a rifle cut off the rest of her words. In the next instant, a bullet ricocheted off the entrance to the cave only inches from her shoulder.

Chapter 9

They didn't wait for a second bullet. With a startled cry, Jessica dived back into the cave. Alex's fierce curses rang in her ears as he also jumped for cover. The metal case holding the money went flying toward the back of the cave, landing with a dull clang. They hardly noticed. Side by side, they leaned against the cave wall, and their ragged breathing seemed loud in the suddenly hushed silence.

Jessica fought back the hysteria threatening to choke her. "We're getting pretty good at dodging bullets."

"If we weren't, we'd be dead by now. Stay here." Steely determination turned the hard lines of Alex's face rigid. "I'll be right back."

Alarmed, she grabbed at him, but he was already cautiously edging toward the rifles they'd left propped just inside the cave entrance. He'd be well within sight of the sharpshooter hiding in the cliffs. She paled. "No!"

Horrified, she watched him tense, his eyes unwavering on the rifles. He sprang, grabbing them just as another shot rang out, and this time the bullet nearly parted his hair.

"Alex!"

He dived toward her, cursing as his shoulder came into contact with a jagged edge of the cave wall. Dragging in a shuddering breath, he lay for a minute with his eyes closed, relief washing through him. When he felt Jessica drop to her knees beside him, he opened one eye. "That was close."

"Close?" she echoed furiously. "Damn it, it almost had your name on it!"

Grabbing her hand, he gave it a quick squeeze. "Don't worry, I have no intention of getting myself killed. But I think it's time we found out who our visitor is. He's wearing out his welcome damn quick."

His hazel eyes were cold, determined, ruthless. Jessica shivered. "Be careful," she whispered.

"Oh, I intend to." Coming to his feet, he handed Jessica her rifle, then slowly crept back toward the cave entrance, making sure to stay out of sight of whoever was hiding in the cliffs. Jessica moved behind him like a shadow, and he motioned to the rocky bluff to the right of the cave entrance. "From the angle of the shots, I'd say they came from over there.

Let's find out." Cupping his hand around his mouth, he yelled, "What do you want?"

"You know what I want," Dutch's familiar raspy voice called back coldly. "The money."

Stunned, Alex uttered a short, bitter obscenity. "Damn that old man! He knows! But how?"

Jessica peered around his shoulder to stare out at the cliffs, but the prospector was clever enough to stay out of sight. "Maybe someone at the prison overheard you and Harlan," she suggested.

He shook his head. "No, Harlan was too careful for that. That money's his ticket out, and he made damn sure no one heard us." Alex's expression was hard and ruthless, and his fingers tightened on his rifle. "I'm not going to let some crazy old codger who talks to mules rob him of his freedom now." Turning back to the cave entrance, he called out, "I've only got twenty bucks, Dutch, and it's yours if you want it. It's not worth dying over."

The old man laughed with unholy glee. "You can save the bull, Trent. When I heard Harlan had cancer, I knew it was just a matter of time before he told someone where he hid the money. I've been following you ever since you left Phoenix."

"How do you know about Harlan?" he demanded. "Who are you?"

"You mean you haven't figured it out yet?" the disembodied voice taunted, chuckling evilly. "The name's Joe Maitland, and that's my three million you found. I've been searching for it for thirteen years, and I mean to have it. If you throw down your guns and come out with your hands up, I'll let you and the woman walk out of here alive.''

Alex felt as if he'd been kicked in the gut. *"Mait-land!"* he whispered hoarsely. "Damn!"

Jessica clutched at his arm. "Joe Maitland! Didn't you say he was—"

"One of Harlan's partners," Alex said coldly. "The one who killed the bank guards."

"But I thought he was in Brazil."

"So did the police," Alex retorted bitterly. "I underestimated the bastard. Harlan warned me to watch out for him. I should have known he'd have spies at the prison watching Harlan's every move."

"Did you hear me, Trent?" the old man yelled impatiently. "You've got ten seconds to come out or—"

"Or what?" Alex called back. "You're going to kill us no matter what, so why should I make it easy for you? If you want the money, come and get it!"

A scatter of rifle fire sprayed the cave entrance. "If that's the way you want it," Maitland roared. "It's your funeral!"

It would be if they didn't figure a way to get out of there. His mind working furiously, Alex fired a defiant shot at the rocks where he knew the old man was hiding. Before he realized Jessica's intentions, she sprinted across to the other side of the cave. His head snapped around. "Damn it, Jessica, get to the back of the cave where it's safe!"

"Not on your life," she retorted. She added her rifle fire to his, peppering the cliff so that the old man was trapped as effectively as they were.

They stopped in unspoken agreement; the silence that settled over the cave and the surrounding cliffs was deadly in its intensity. Her heart still in her throat, Jessica glanced over at Alex's scowling face and managed an impudent grin. The lift of her chin was all too familiar to him. "Well, this is a fine mess you've gotten us into. Now what?"

Though he was still irritated that she refused to move back to a safer position he couldn't help but grin. "You have got to be the most stubborn woman I ever met in my life."

"I'll take that as a compliment, if you don't mind."

"I figured you would." He chuckled, then suddenly sobered, his eyes drifting to the cliffs before returning to hers. "We're going to have to get out of this by ourselves, you know. Charlie will never make it back in time to help us."

She'd already come to that same conclusion. "Do you really think he'd kill us if we turned the money over to him?"

"He'd put a bullet between your eyes the minute you stepped outside," he said flatly. "He must have been scouring these mountains for the last thirteen years looking for that money. Now that he's almost got his hands on it again he's sure as hell not going to let us stop him."

Glancing outside, he frowned. They'd been in the cave longer than he'd realized. The sun had already sunk behind the mountains. It would be dark in a little over an hour, and they'd have to make their move. "As soon as it's dark, we're going to slip out of here and circle back to camp for the horses," he told her grimly. "We'll lose him in the dark."

"And probably get ourselves killed in the process!" she exclaimed, horrified at his suggestion. "You can't really expect to *ride* out of here?"

"It beats getting shot," he retorted, stung. Damn it, if John Wayne rode to the rescue right now, she'd argue with him! "If you've got a better idea, let's hear it."

"Have you forgotten it rained last night?" she demanded.

Suddenly memories of the night before seemed to materialize between them, reminding them of the loving they had yet to speak of, and she wanted to bite off her tongue. Heat climbed into her cheeks. "The mountain trails are dangerous enough during the daytime," she said stiffly. "To take them on horseback on a dark night after a rain would be sheer madness. We'd never make it."

She was right. He leaned his head against the rock wall at his back and closed his eyes. "We can't stay here. We've got Maitland trapped for now, but as soon as it's dark he's going to come after us. We can't let him trap us in this cave."

"Then we'll have to walk out," she said determinedly. "It's the only choice we've got."

The next hour seemed to pass with agonizing slowness. Jessica and Alex sat Indian-style on the cave floor. Their rifles rested across their knees, and they seldom took their eyes off the cliffs opposite the cave entrance. Nothing moved, but they hadn't really expected it to. Maitland was no fool. He, too, was waiting for nightfall.

Alex dragged his eyes away from the sky, which was growing darker with every passing minute. Jessica sat in the shadows, but he could see the paleness of her face, and the tension that turned her delicate figure to stone. He'd brought her to this, he thought in disgust, and there wasn't a hell of a lot he could do about it now. Settling back against the rock wall behind him, he asked quietly, "How many ways are there out of the mountains?"

She jumped, then cursed her revealing skittishness. "Three," she said huskily. "The way we came in's the fastest."

"If Maitland's been searching these mountains for the last thirteen years, then he'll know that, too. He'll probably be waiting for us there. What about the other two?"

"There's a trail that starts west of the springs. It's the easiest, but miles out of the way. It would take forever on foot."

"And once Maitland figures out we didn't take the fast way, he'll come after us on horseback once the sun comes up." They'd be sitting ducks. The odds were getting worse and worse. Muttering an oath under his breath, he asked, "Looks like we'll have to take the last one and hope he doesn't catch on to us until it's too late. What is it?"

Jessica paled. "Over the escarpment at the other end of the canyon."

A muscle ticked along Alex's jaw. The escarpment. A thousand feet of sheer rock that formed the last barrier between the mountains and the desert. No wonder she was pale. A climb of that magnitude in the dark would be suicidal, but it was the only chance they had. Maitland was overweight and well into his sixties. Even if he thought they were crazy enough to try the cliffs, the chances of his following them were slim.

"It's the only way, Jessica. We've got to take it."

Her eyes, blank and unseeing, settled on the growing darkness outside. When she finally spoke, her voice was empty. "My husband died up there."

After slipping out of her hands, Alex thought, his expression grave as he remembered the memories she'd sobbed out on his shoulder. The guilt of that day still had the power to haunt her, and he was asking her to step into the nightmare.

But what else could he do?

"I'm sorry," he said gruffly, aching to hold her. "But we don't have any other choice. The only chance in hell we've got of getting out of these mountains alive is over that escarpment."

She knew he was right, but the thought of climbing up those cliffs sickened her. If something happened, she wouldn't be able to stand it again. Unknowingly, she voiced her fears by her silence.

"Don't worry," Alex growled. "If we're lucky enough to get out of this cave without getting shot,

I'm sure as hell not going to let these mountains defeat us. We'll make it.''

Jessica wanted to believe him, but when night finally covered the mountains she wasn't ready for it. The gradually darkening shadows silently invaded the cave. Then they moved to the canyon outside, filling it until the only light was a dim glow that clung to the highest peaks and ridges.

Alex stood abruptly, only seconds before the darkness became infernal, and stripped off his black T-shirt. At Jessica's start of surprise, he said, ''You can't wear that white shirt. Maitland would spot you the minute you stepped outside.'' He tossed her his T-shirt. ''Wear this,'' he said huskily.

Her heart pounding, she curled her fingers around the soft cotton still warm from his body. His scent swirled around her to tease her senses. If she lived to be a hundred, she didn't think she'd ever forget his faintly spicy, masculine smell.

Her fingers moved to the buttons of her blouse, and suddenly the tension in the cave had nothing to do with the danger outside. She could hardly see his face, but she knew his eyes were on her, following the trail of her fingers, remembering. Heat licked at her. Swallowing painfully, she finally slipped her blouse from her shoulders and let it fall to the ground. Even in the darkness, she could see the glint in his eyes. Could he hear the pounding of her heart?

Did she have any idea what she was doing to him? he wondered with a groan. Watching her pull his T-shirt on was slow, exquisite torture. Last night he'd lost himself in her arms so completely that he'd been sure he'd never need her quite that much again. But the desire was back, stronger than before. Too powerful to be merely physical, too enticing to be safe. How could he ever have thought that one night of loving her would be enough for him?

Clenching his jaw on a frustrated curse, he dragged his eyes back to the cave opening and saw the last of the light disappear. "It's time," he said tightly. "Let's go."

Jessica sensed rather than saw him grab his rifle and the case that held the money before he moved to the cave entrance. Panic knotted her stomach. This was it. Do or die. Bracing herself for whatever would greet them once they stepped outside, she silently moved to his side. When he looked down at her inquiringly in the darkness, she pointed to their left, away from the camp. From now on there would be no talking until they were well away from the cave and the man who hunted them.

The first step out of the cave was the hardest. Holding her breath, Jessica moved behind Alex like a shadow as he slipped outside. The hammering of her heart deafened her as the darkness and silence of the canyon enveloped them.

Nothing moved.

The relief lasted the span of a heartbeat. The darkness freed Maitland as much as it did them. If they were going to get out of here alive, it was up to her. Gathering her courage, Jessica took the lead.

They slipped silently through the darkness like cats running free in the night.

The long hours that followed were something out of a nightmare. There was no moon to guide them, only Jessica's tortured memories. They dodged her every footstep, mocking her, taunting her, refusing to retreat to the past where they belonged. She knew that Maitland could be anywhere in the darkness, sniffing out their trail, waiting for the chance to ambush them in the night. But it was the escarpment that made her break out in a cold sweat. The escarpment that struck terror to her heart. With every step, she drew closer to it.

Suddenly it was in front of her. She felt Alex come up behind her, but her eyes were on the black, forbidding countenance of the mountain that towered above them and seemed to disappear into the night. It looked as smooth and unbroken as a sheet of ebony glass, but Jessica knew the imposing precipice was actually a series of individual cliffs stacked one on top of another, connected by ledges that couldn't be seen from the canyon floor. There was no such thing as a path leading to the top, only handholds, hidden pockets the rain and wind had carved out of the rock over the centuries. It wasn't a climb for the fainthearted.

She'd been twelve years old when she'd first conquered the escarpment. She'd been scared even then, but at that age the challenge it had presented had impressed her far more than the fear. Beating it had been like flying without a plane—exhilarating. Her grandfather hadn't been pleased, and Charlie had thrown a fit when he'd learned what she'd done, but it had been days before she'd come down from the high of her accomplishment.

She'd thought then that she'd never be afraid of the escarpment again. Then her husband had died and she'd learned that the mountains always won in the end.

She turned to Alex, her eyes eloquent with emotion as they found his in the darkness. She wanted to tell him that this was a mistake. She wasn't a reckless twelve-year-old any more; she knew better than most how the mountains could snuff out a life before you could blink.

The words trembled on her tongue, but before she could speak, he gently laid his finger against her lips and shook his head slightly. With a touch as gentle as a kiss, his hand moved over her cheek and around to the back of her neck, tunneling under the black cloud of her hair to pull her soundlessly to him and bury her face against his throat. For a timeless moment he just held her, wordlessly offering her the comfort of his body.

Jessica shuddered against him and closed her eyes with a sigh, wondering how he'd known she'd needed just to be held. She hadn't known it herself, and it wasn't a need she let herself acknowledge very often. Then again, he seemed to have a talent for discovering, then satisfying, her needs. Dear God, what was she going to do when he was gone?

Alex could have cursed at whatever thought had her pulling out of his arms and destroying the sweetness of the moment. He searched her face, but her emotions were carefully concealed. She was still pale, but her chin was lifted in that independent way of hers. When she turned toward the cliffs, he had no choice but to follow.

From then on, Joe Maitland and the rest of the world ceased to exist. There was nothing but the two of them silently fighting the mountains, struggling against an enemy they could hardly see but could always feel.

Jagged edges, unseen in the night, scraped their hands raw and tore at their clothes and unprotected skin. They climbed for what seemed like hours, until they ached in every muscle and only sheer strength of will kept them going. They pushed on from sheer desperation and the knowledge that there was nowhere else to go but up.

Sometime between her husband's death and now, the route Jessica had mapped out as a child had altered. Whole sections of the cliff had apparently fallen to the canyon below, changing everything. She was left to search in the dark for handholds, feeling her way across the cliff like a blind woman exploring her lover's face for the first time.

After endless hours of searching, of having to backtrack because the route they'd taken had turned into a dead end, they stumbled onto a ledge that was only thirty feet away from the top of the escarpment. Relief coursed through her, suddenly making her aware of just how exhausted she was. Rest. Her body ached for it. But she couldn't stop now, not when they were so close to winning. They'd take a break at the top.

She found a depression in the rock, then another, climbing steadily. Her eyes were trained on the dark summit she could barely see outlined against the night sky.

Without warning, gravel rolled underfoot, and suddenly there was nothing under her feet but thin, black air waiting to swallow her up.

She screamed, her rifle tumbling from her shoulders to the canyon floor below, and clutched wildly for a crack in the rock to wedge her hands into. Pain raced like wildfire across her shoulders as her arms took her full weight. "Alex!"

He was still on the ledge below her, and his head jerked up at her cry of horror. His heart stopped at the sight of her clinging to the side of the cliff. "Hang on!" he cried hoarsely. "I'm coming. *Don't let go!*"

Later he couldn't remember scrambling up the side of the cliff after her, but suddenly he was just below her, his head at her knees as he hovered protectively behind her. "I've got you," he promised thickly, wincing as the metal case of money he'd strapped to his back with his belt pulled at him like an anchor. "Let go and you'll slide down until your feet are resting on the top of mine."

She whimpered, her heart slamming against her ribs. Her fingers were freezing, and nightmares of the past flashed obscenely in her head. Hot tears squeezed out from behind her tightly clenched eyelids to spill onto the rough rock where her cheek rested. "I—I c-can't."

"Yes, you can," he said urgently. "You can do anything you set your mind to. I'm right below you, ready to catch you. Trust me. I'd never let anything happen to you."

She'd known that from the very beginning, and she'd fought him every step of the way because of it. But how could she deny the truth when he stood between her and certain death? She could trust him with her heart, her life.

She caught her breath on a sob, torn between tears and an insane urge to laugh. God, what a crazy time to discover she loved him!

"Jess?"

The soft, worried calling of her name snapped the hysteria threatening to choke her. She swallowed. "I—I'm okay. How far is it back down to the ledge?"

"About eight feet. But first you're going to slide down to me. Ready?" He could just barely see her nod her head. He braced himself, digging his fingers into the rock. "All right, drop!"

Sending up a silent prayer, she relaxed her fingers with painstaking slowness, releasing their hold. In the next instant she was sliding down the weathered rock, and there was hardly time for her to feel the terror of falling before he brought her to a jarring stop, taking her weight. She gasped and felt his body cover hers completely, his heart pounding against her back. It was the sweetest feeling she'd ever known.

Alex buried his face in her hair, a shudder ripping through him. Too close, he thought furiously. He'd come too damn close to losing her! Raw emotions pulled at him, tearing him apart, and for a moment it was all he could do to remember that he was in no position to crush her in his arms. She was safe for now, but she'd never have been in danger if he hadn't dragged her into it. He wouldn't blame her if she hated him.

Lifting his face, he said tightly, "Now we're going to work our way down to the ledge, starting with my right foot. One step at a time. All you've got to do is move with me. Okay?"

She nodded. At that moment, he could have said they were going to walk on water and she wouldn't have argued with him. "I'm ready when you are."

She felt him tense, the muscles in his legs and arms constricting along hers, and then he was quietly guiding her through each step, his voice a murmur in her ear, warm, encouraging.

"Ready? Right first. Easy!" His breath ruffled her hair. "Now left. That's it. You're doing fine."

It only took minutes to reach the ledge, but they were the longest minutes of their lives. Their muscles quivered with the strain of keeping their movements slow and cautious, and by the time Alex brought them to a halt on firm ground they were both drenched in sweat. For a moment they just stood there, surprise quickly giving way to a gush of giddy relief.

They were safe.

Her heart still beating erratically in her breast, Jessica only took time to give Alex a laughing hug before she was turning to the cliff again, her fingers blindly searching for another route to the top. But the rock was as smooth as glass; the only depression where she could gain a hold was the one she'd discovered earlier.

The irony of their situation hit her just before the panic. They couldn't go any farther without taking the route she'd just tried, and if they went down they were right back in Joe Maitland's clutches. Either way could spell certain death.

They were trapped.

"No!" she cried, frantically running her hands over the face of the cliff again. "There has to be a way out! Damn it, we're so close. We can't stop here!"

Alex frowned at her stricken words and quickly moved to help her search. "Calm down, sweetheart. We've haven't come this far to stop now. We'll find a way out."

His confidence, far from reassuring her, only snapped her control. Fear, anger, panic exploded in a burst of hot words. She glared at him in the darkness, not even feeling the tears running down her cheeks. "How? By sprouting wings and flying out of here? That's about the only chance we've got. Every time we think we're winning, the mountains knock us down again. I hate them! Do you hear me? I hate them! I wish to God I'd never stepped foot—"

Alex didn't wait to hear the rest. He grabbed her, hauling her against him and trapping her flailing arms between their bodies when she tried to strike out at him. She was shaking, angry tears coursing down her face. The struggle to push out of his arms lasted all of a second before she suddenly wilted against him and gave in to the misery choking her.

Stunned, Alex dragged her closer, her pain destroying him. She hadn't shed a tear when she'd been nearly crushed by a boulder, she'd hardly flinched when a bullet had almost killed her, and even when she'd been dangling from the side of the cliff she'd fought the mountain, refusing to give in to defeat. But now that they were almost over the top, she was crying as if her heart were breaking.

His arms tightened around her. "Oh, sweetheart, don't," he pleaded. "I promise you it's going to be all right." Murmuring to her soothingly, he pressed a kiss to her brow, her cheek, and tasted the saltiness of her tears on his lips. "Please don't cry," he groaned. "I can't stand it when you cry."

"I can't h-help it!"

He couldn't help but grin at her sniffling indignation. Burying his fingers in her hair, he dragged her head back so he could see her shadowed face. Tears glistened in the darkness. "If you keep this up, we'll be able to float out of here on a river of tears."

She sniffed. "I *hate* to cry!"

"I don't know why. You do it very well."

"Damn it, Alex, how can you joke at a time like this? We're stuck up here."

"No, we're not." He turned her back to the cliff and touched a crack in the rock just beyond her fingertips. It opened into a fissure that, unless he missed his guess, led all the way to the top. His hands settled at her waist, lifting her easily. "There's an opening right there," he said, motioning to the spot, just inches above her fingers. "Feel it?" At her gasp, he laughed. "Still think the mountains are going to win?" he teased, and hoisted her up to the foothold and freedom.

Chapter 10

Their exhilaration when they reached the top was quickly followed by an exhaustion that was so enervating that it threatened to buckle Jessica's knees. She ached in every bone in her body, and her hands felt as if she'd been stringing barbed wire without gloves. She'd have liked nothing better than to sink down to the rocky ground and close her eyes for a minute, just a minute. But if she did she might not be able to get up again, and they weren't home free yet. The path down the other side of the mountains was just as steep and treacherous as the route they'd forged up the cliffs. They couldn't afford to relax their guard for even a second.

After that, it was only the wild, arid scent of the desert and the knowledge that her land started at the

foot of the mountains that kept Jessica moving. Night
faded into dawn and then into morning, and once
again the sun baked the land. She was too tired to
notice, too tired to care. Every step became a test of
endurance as her feet turned leaden and her mind
clouded with the sheer effort of moving, always
moving. Hours passed, seeming like days. She didn't
feel the sun burn her skin or the wind chap her lips.
She concentrated so wholly on just lifting her foot for
the next step that she didn't see the rock in the middle of the trail until it was too late.

She stumbled, and if Alex hadn't been so close behind her, he wouldn't have caught her. He moved like
lightning, jerking her against him with a muttered
oath before she could tumble down the mountain.
"Easy, love," he breathed roughly against his hair.
"You didn't come all this way to break your neck
when the end's in sight."

She blinked, leaning tiredly against him, her eyes
closing in a frown. "The end?"

He chuckled. "Your ranch. Don't you see it?"

Her bleary eyes popped open. The ranch. It was
spread out before her like a mirage on the desert floor,
the tin roofs of the outbuildings glistening in the
midday sun. A sudden rush of foolish tears blinded
her. She'd cried more in the last few days than she had
in years, but she couldn't find the strength to stop.
She was almost home. Safe. After the nightmare
they'd just been through, could she even remember
the definition of the word?

The arm around her waist tightened as Alex peered around her shoulder to get a good look at her face. "Hey, you're not going to cry again, are you?" he teased, his dimples flashing rakishly. "I'm still waterlogged from the last time. Not that I'm complaining," he quickly amended. "A woman's supposed to lean on a man. She can't help it if she's weaker—umph!"

Her elbow caught him in the chest. Her grin was tired but cocky as her eyes met his. "You were saying?" she asked archly, knowing she hadn't hurt him.

"I thought that would snap you out of it," he laughed, wondering if she had any idea just how beautiful she looked standing there in his T-shirt with dirt streaking her face. With her hair tumbling about her shoulders and clinging to the curve of her cheek and her sapphire eyes now free of tears and as clear as the morning sky, she looked as wild as the mountains.

God, he wanted her! Here. Now. With nothing but the mountains around them and the warm desert air brushing their naked skin. Just one last time before they went back to her ranch and the time they'd spent together faded into a memory.

But even as he recognized the desire heating his blood, it was too late. The real world had already intruded. He could see by her eyes that the ranch was claiming her. Her sons and the responsibilities she'd left were tugging at her. And he had his own responsibilities, he reminded himself. Harlan was counting the days, waiting for his return. Time was running out.

He released her, the smile falling from his face. "We'd better be going. Maitland knows by now that we got away. We've got to notify the sheriff before he can disappear again, and then I've got to get back to Phoenix. I've already been gone too long as it is."

The pain that lanced her heart was swift and brutal. So he was leaving as soon as possible. Why was she so surprised, so hurt? she thought furiously. He'd gone into the mountains for just one thing, and now that he had it he had no need of her. If she'd remembered that from the very beginning, her heart wouldn't be breaking now.

Lifting her chin proudly, she said, "Then it's a good thing we came over the escarpment. You'll be home two days early."

She whirled before he could say another word and started down the trail again, quickening her pace to outdistance her tortured thoughts. Her exhausted muscles screamed in protest. She could hear Alex swearing as he hurried to keep up with her, but she couldn't slow down. She was falling apart on the inside, and if she didn't get to the ranch soon she was going to make a complete fool of herself.

An hour later she quietly stepped through the back door into the kitchen. Alex was close behind her. At the familiar sight of Charlie and Mary Lou lingering over lunch, she blinked back tears and grinned. "Is there enough for two more, or did you guys eat it all?"

Her two oldest friends looked at her as if they'd just seen a ghost. Mary Lou set her iced tea down with a bang, her eyes dark with concern as she noted Jessica's scratched and sunburned cheeks, the exhaustion weighing heavily on her shoulders and the silent, somber man who stood behind her dressed in nothing but jeans, tennis shoes and an overnight growth of beard.

"Good Lord, are you all right?" she exclaimed, jumping up to rush over to them. "Here, sit down. You both look like you're ready to drop."

"They look like they've been in a fight," Charlie growled, hurrying to pull out two chairs for them. His sharp eyes narrowed at the sight of the metal case strapped to Alex's back like a backpack. "You found it," he said grimly.

"Yesterday afternoon," Alex said as he eased the straps off his shoulders and lowered the case to the floor at his feet.

"Yesterday!" the older man echoed, astonished. "How the hell did you get here so fast? I got caught in that damn storm and didn't get in until yesterday afternoon myself."

Mary Lou shot him a quick frown of disapproval. "Give them a chance to catch their breath," she said from the stove as she hastily dished up lunch for them. Setting the full plates in front of them, she moved to the refrigerator for the iced tea. "They look like they've been up all night."

"We have," Jessica said, reaching for her fork as the first hunger pangs hit her. "Where are the boys?"

"John's out riding, and Matthew and Mark are hunting out a new litter of kittens in the barn." Grinning in satisfaction as she watched Jessica and Alex dig into their food, Mary Lou took the chair at the end of the table and asked, "When's the last time you two ate?"

"Lunch yesterday," Alex admitted, then took a long, thirst-quenching drink.

Clearly impatient, Charlie couldn't wait any longer to satisfy his curiosity. "All right, spit it out. How'd you manage to get here so fast, and why haven't you eaten since yesterday?"

Jessica met his fierce gaze without flinching. "We had to get out of the mountains fast and the only way out was over the escarpment."

He turned pale under his weathered tan. "At night? Damn it, what were you trying to do? Kill yourselves?"

"We didn't have to try the cliffs to do that," she retorted. "We had a visitor who was perfectly willing to do it for us."

"Who?"

"Our old prospecting friend, Dutch," Alex said flatly. "Only that's not his real name. Thirteen years ago he was known as Joseph Maitland. He was one of Harlan's partners."

"Son of a bitch!" Charlie swore. "Are you sure?"

Jessica nodded. "We got it straight from the horse's mouth. It seems he's been hiding out in the mountains all these years and nobody even gave him a second look."

Mary Lou frowned in exasperation. "Would somebody like to start at the beginning and tell me what's going on? Charlie said Slim was found at the bottom of a ravine and nobody knows how he got there. What's this money you're talking about? And who's Maitland?"

Alex quickly filled her in, explaining everything. "Maitland knew Harlan was dying and was bound to tell someone about the money," he said twenty minutes later as he finished the story. "I was the only visitor he'd had in the last six months, so Maitland figured all he had to do was follow me and I'd lead him right to the money."

"The whole time we were digging out in the heat, he was probably sitting up there in the rocks watching us," Jessica added in disgust. "The minute we came out of the cave with the money, he was ready to pick us off like fish in a barrel."

"My God." Mary Lou gasped. "He's a crafty son of a gun, isn't he?"

"He hasn't avoided arrest the last thirteen years by being stupid," Alex agreed. "This was his first mistake, and if I don't report this to the sheriff, he's going to get away again."

He came purposefully to his feet, obviously anxious to be on his way, his eyes on the yellow wall phone near the back door. Jessica felt the despair sink into her stomach and forced a smile. "Use the phone in my office. You can put the money in my safe until you turn it over to the sheriff."

After showing him to her office and locking the money away, she quietly left him to his call and returned to the kitchen just as the back door squeaked open. Mark and Matthew ran in with a newborn kitten under each arm and almost dropped them at the sight of her.

"Mom!"

With a cry of joy, they dumped the kittens in Charlie's lap and practically tripped over each other to get to Jessica first. Hugging her madly, they laughed as she collapsed into the nearest chair with them in her arms.

"We didn't think you'd be back for days. How come you're back early?"

"How'd you get those scrapes on your cheeks? And whose T-shirt is that? Are you okay, Mom? You don't look so good."

"Wait, wait!" She chuckled, drawing them to her for a desperate hug. How she had missed them! "I got back early because Alex found what he was looking for. The T-shirt is his, and I'm fine. Where's your brother?"

"Still out riding," Matthew said with shrug.

She ruffled his hair playfully. "So what happened while I was gone? Did you guys keep out of trouble?"

"Of course!" he said indignantly.

"Mary Lou let us make cookies," Mark added. "She said they were the best she ever ate!"

"You burned yours," Matthew reminded him.

"He comes by that naturally," Charlie said dryly, his green eyes twinkling.

Mary Lou chuckled. "That was the day Pete put the new well in, and letting them make cookies distracted them for a while. Though by the time poor Pete got out of here, he was looking pretty frazzled."

The well, Jessica thought dazedly. In all the excitement, she'd almost forgotten it! "So he found water? When? Did he have any problems?"

"Not a one," the housekeeper assured her. "You know Pete. He's got a nose for water. Hardly had to drill at all before he struck a doozy of a well. Said to tell you you shouldn't have to worry about water for years."

She sighed in relief. If the drilling had gone as easily as Mary Lou said, then the trip into the mountains had been worth it. She'd earned more than enough to pay Pete's bill in full. But would she ever be able to turn on the tap without thinking of Alex?

Charlie watched shadows of pain cloud her eyes and frowned. "You all right, Jessie? You didn't hurt yourself coming over those damned cliffs, did you?"

"No. I'm f-fine. Just tired." Suddenly needing to be alone with her thoughts, she gave the boys another quick hug before coming abruptly to her feet and heading for the kitchen doorway. "I've got to get some sleep—"

"Easy," Alex cautioned, stepping into the doorway at the same time and almost running into her. His hands settled at her waist, and the look in his eyes was unconsciously intimate. "You okay?"

Okay? she thought wildly. How could she be okay when suddenly just breathing was difficult? Struggling to regain the control that was quickly deserting her, she stepped back, away from his touch. "I'm f-fine. Did you talk to the sheriff?"

Impatience flickered in his eyes. "No. It seems there's been a train derailment on the other side of town. The dispatcher wasn't sure how serious it was, but she said it could be hours before the sheriff's free. It's still not safe for anyone to get wind of the money, so I just had to leave a message for him to come out to the ranch as soon as possible."

So he would be stuck here for at least a few more hours, possibly more. It wasn't nearly enough for her, but it was obviously too much for him. "If you're that anxious to leave, why don't you just drive into town and give the information to one of his assistants?"

His eyes narrowed at her tone. He didn't want to leave. There were too many things left unsaid. They both needed time to come to grips with what had happened in the mountains, and time was something he had precious little of now. He'd called his secretary and learned that Harlan's condition had worsened.

"I'm not anxious to carry around three million dollars," he retorted. "And since he needs to talk to you, too, I might as well wait for him here. I'll leave after that."

The tension that invaded the kitchen was almost tangible. Mary Lou cleared her throat and took charge. "Well, then, you've both got time to clean up and probably even catch up on some sleep before Jake gets here. Jessica, why don't you show Alex to the guest room." Without waiting for an answer, she turned to the boys. "Weren't you guys going to clean out the barn today?" she asked them.

"But John's not here!" they chorused in unison. "That's not fair!"

"He'll help you as soon as he gets back. Besides," she coaxed, "if you get your work done earlier, you can go up to the creek for a swim."

That was all the encouragement they needed. Whooping with glee, they stopped just long enough to collect the kittens from Charlie before they hit the back door at a dead run, letting it slam behind them. Mary Lou turned to Jessica with a satisfied grin on her lined face. "That ought to keep them busy for a couple of hours. You two better get up those stairs while you still can. I'll call you if the sheriff comes before you come down."

Jessica left Alex in the guest room with clean towels and some clothes borrowed from some of the ranch hands. She hastily escaped to her own room. She meant to linger in the bathtub, to wash her hair, then just lie in the hot water and let the heat seep into her tired muscles. But the minute she slipped into the tub she was suddenly reminded of the mountain spring and Alex. She could see again his face as he'd

stepped under the trees and seen her in the spring's
bubbling water, feel again the almost physical stroking of his eyes. Suddenly her bathwater was impossibly hot, and any thoughts of lingering vanished into
the steam that swirled above her head. Sighing, she
reached for a towel and quickly dried herself before
pulling on a nightshirt and hurrying into her bedroom, determined to lose her painful memories in
sleep.

Her mind, however, had other ideas. Her head had
hardly touched the pillow before she was asleep and
in Alex's arms, the memory of his loving teasing her
until her blood ran hot through her veins and a sweet
ache settled deep inside her. She reached for him,
wanting more, needing more—and touched only
emptiness.

She woke with a start, stared at her outstretched
arm and closed her eyes on a groan of despair. He
hadn't even left yet, and she was already missing him.
Dear God, how was she going to go back to the life
she'd been content with before he'd shown up in her
barn? She had only to look up at the mountains to be
reminded of him, had only to hear the rumble of
thunder in a distant storm to hear his voice in the
wind. And every time she pulled on a cotton nightshirt she'd feel his hands pulling it from her.

Stop it! she told herself sharply. She knew better
than most that this wasn't the way to get over a man.
It took work, lots of hard work that left her so tired
at the end of the day she wouldn't be able to think, let
alone feel.

Jumping out of bed, she jerked off her nightshirt and quickly pulled on jeans and a chambray shirt before stomping into her boots. She'd catch up on the books. She'd always hated that part of ranch work, but it would keep her mind occupied.

Running lightly down the stairs, her black hair flying out behind her, she came to an abrupt halt at the bottom, her eyes wide. Alex lay stretched out on his stomach on the living room rug in his borrowed jeans and work shirt. His bent elbow rested on the rug and his hand was in the air. Alex was ready to Indian-wrestle. Directly across from him, Matthew lay in the same position, his blue eyes fierce with concentration as they locked with Alex's. "This time I'm going to beat you!"

Alex grinned and clasped his hand in a firm grip, breaking eye contact only long enough to glance at Mark, who sat Indian-style next to them, his elbows resting on his knees as he watched them like a hawk. "Call it, Mark."

"One, two, three . . . go!"

Matthew gritted his teeth, the muscles in his arm rippling as he tried with all his strength to pull Alex's hand down to the rug. Mark yelled encouragement, and for a moment it looked as if Matthew were going to win. Jessica watched his eyes widen with excitement, but in the next instant their positions were reversed. Alex won in a flash, drawing groans of defeat from the boys.

"Aw, Matthew, you almost had him!"

Grinning, Alex sat up. "You guys are tough to beat! Who taught you to Indian-wrestle?"

"Mom," Matthew answered proudly. "She says we're getting harder to beat every year."

"That's right," Jessica chuckled, drawing their eyes to where she stood at the foot of the stairs. "I'm going to have to start lifting weights or something so I won't lose."

"You're strong for a girl, Mom," Mark said with the innocent chauvinism of a nine-year-old. "But girls can't help it 'cause they're weak—"

"Those are fighting words, Mark," Alex warned him, laughing at Jessica's lifted brow. "Better watch it."

Her eyes twinkled. "That's right. You keep talking like that and I just might get Matthew to dunk you when you go swimming this afternoon. Did you finish cleaning out the barn?"

"Yep. All done."

"And John didn't even come back and help us. Next time he has to do it by himself."

She frowned, glancing into the kitchen. "You mean he's not back yet?"

"Oh, you know how he is, Mom," Matthew said. "He probably stopped at the creek for a drink and stayed there all afternoon daydreaming. Do we have to wait for him to get back before we go swimming? Can't we meet him up there?"

Jessica hesitated, a frown worrying her brow before she reluctantly gave in. "Oh, I guess so. But be careful!'' she called as they sprinted up the stairs to change.

Alex watched them disappear upstairs, then he glanced over at Jessica. ''Do they do everything at full speed ahead?''

''Just about,'' she chuckled. ''They were born a month and a half early, and they've been in a hurry ever since.''

And all these years she'd been their sole support, he thought, marveling again at what she must have gone through. Not only had she had the responsibility of the boys, she had also had the ranch. And the cattle industry had been in trouble for some time now. She'd have had to work her fingers to the bone just to keep her head above water. How had she managed everything without going quietly out of her mind?

''The sheriff should be here soon,'' he said gruffly. ''Before he gets here, I'd like to settle up with you on what I owe you.'' He didn't notice the stricken look in her eyes as he pulled his wallet from his back pocket. ''There's a reward for the recovery of the money, and half of that is yours. As soon as it comes through, I'll get it to you,'' he promised, handing her a neat stack of hundred-dollar bills. ''This is for your guide services.''

Jessica took it numbly. She'd known this moment was coming, the time when he thanked her and prepared to leave. But God, she wasn't ready for it! She wasn't going to be able to stand quietly by and watch him leave. Not without asking him to stay.

''Alex—''

"Jessica!" The back door slamming behind him, Charlie charged into the living room, his whiskered face gray beneath his tan, his green eyes dark with fear. "Jessie, honey..."

She paled at the quiet desperation she heard in his voice and clutched at his arm. "What is it, Charlie? Tell me!"

He swallowed, and his words, when he finally found them, were rough with pain. "John's horse came back to the barn without him. He must have taken a fall somewhere."

John. Of the three boys he was the baby, a tease, an instigator, an explorer—and the one she worried about the most. He knew the ranch like the back of his hand. But sometimes when he was riding he got caught up in daydreaming and didn't always pay attention to what he was doing.

Panic threatened, but she couldn't, wouldn't, give in to it. Not yet. Dragging in a calming breath, she said, "He's taken spills before. We'll just have to go out and find him."

Charlie nodded and immediately headed for the back door. "I'll round up the rest of the hands, and we'll start searching as soon as we saddle up. You gonna take the truck?"

"Yes. I'll check all his favorite spots. I ... I'm sure he's fine."

"I'm coming with you," Alex said grimly, stepping forward to pry the money she was crushing out of her fingers. "I'll put this in your office while you get the keys to the truck."

She blinked and suddenly remembered he was leaving as soon as he could. "Alex, you don't have to—"

"I *want* to," he said tightly. "Okay?"

"But the sheriff—"

"Mary Lou will explain." Turning her around so that her back was to him, he gave her a gentle push. "Quit worrying about me and get your keys."

The next few hours were a nightmare. Charlie and the other hands divided the ranch into four sections and scoured it thoroughly, ignoring the heat and the frustration that grew with every passing second. In her battered pickup, with Alex at her side, Jessica jostled and bumped over the rough terrain, squinting against the sun's glare as her eyes ceaselessly searched the barren landscape. But all she saw were dust devils whipped up by the wind.

John had a dozen or more favorite spots on the ranch, and they checked every one of them—the old Indian hunting ground where he searched for arrowheads, the ridge in the foothills of the mountains that gave a commanding view of the house and barns, the windmill in the north forty, the creek.

There wasn't a sign of him anywhere.

With every spot they checked, Jessica grew more frantic. She hid it well, calmly announcing another place he might be and heading for it, but Alex knew her now and he wasn't fooled. Her fingers bit into the wheel, and her eyes, when he caught a glimpse of them, were nearly black with fear. She was falling apart on the inside, and there wasn't a damn thing he could do about it. God, he loved her!

Love. The word hit him like a blast from a double-barreled shotgun. He'd known from the first moment he'd seen her working in the barn that she was different from the women he knew. Sweeter, tarter, hotter. He should have known then that she was what had been missing from his life, the woman he wanted to spend eternity with. He almost laughed at the thought. This from a man who took pride in not being tied down? The woman had bewitched him!

And she was hurting. He watched her desperation turn to panic and ached to hold her, soothe her. But nothing he could say or do would help nearly as much as finding her son. Vowing to be there for her no matter what, he decided to go along with any plan she had, refusing to kill the last of her hope.

Not content to search the area of the creek where the boys normally swam, she insisted on following it all the way back to the spring where it started, just in case John had decided to go exploring. But he wasn't there, and Alex knew then she'd had enough. The assurances she'd been giving both of them over the last two hours silenced. Giving in to the need to hold her, he pulled her against him. "Let's go back to the house," he said softly. "Charlie or one of the hands has probably already found him and he's waiting for you there."

She couldn't stop herself from clutching at him. "No! We've got to keep looking. If he's hurt—"

She couldn't finish the sentence, and although Alex would have given anything to tell her he was sure John was safe, he couldn't. His arms tightened around her. "If he's not back at the house, then we'll go out looking for him again. We'll find him. We won't stop looking till we do."

It was the most logical thing to do. But if he wasn't there, dear God, what would she do? Throwing off the fear that threatened to swamp her at that thought, she stepped free of his arms while she still could. "You're right. Let's go back to the house."

But the moment they stepped through the back door into the kitchen, Jessica knew John hadn't been found. Charlie and half a dozen ranch hands were gathered around the table, their faces etched with worry, while Mark and Matthew clung to Mary Lou. The instant the children saw Jessica, they flew into her arms, holding her as if they'd never let her go. Over their heads, her tortured eyes met Charlie's. "Charlie?"

"We've combed every inch of this damn ranch, Jessie," he said hoarsely. "And there ain't hide nor hair of that boy anywhere. I can't imagine what happened to him. It's as if he just vanished off the face of the earth!"

"He's got to be somewhere!" she cried desperately. "Did you see what direction his horse came from?"

"The creek. But we checked the creek."

"So did we."

The sudden ringing of the phone shattered the quiet despair that followed her admission. Gently disentangling herself from the boys, she picked up the receiver, ready to tell whoever it was that she couldn't possibly talk now. But the words never left her mouth, because she recognized the cold voice on the other end of the line.

"Mrs. Rawlins, I have your son."

Chapter 11

Did you hear me, Mrs. Rawlins?"

John. Oh, God, he had her son! Somewhere in the back of her mind, a voice told her this wasn't real, *couldn't* be real. But the words still echoed in her head, mocking her, dragging her down into a living nightmare. Fear, cold and deadly, turned her blood to ice. "Is he all right?" she cried. "Damn you, if you hurt him—"

"You'll what?" Maitland snarled. "I'm the one holding all the cards, lady, and if you want to see your son again you'll do as I say. I want my money."

"But—"

"No buts!" he snapped. "I get the dough or your son dies. It's that simple. Are you going to cooperate?"

Rage boiled up in her, every vile name she had ever heard trembling on her tongue. What kind of monster was he that he even had to ask the question? Cooperate? Of course she would cooperate! But if he hurt her child—

Her mind shut down at the thought, enfolding her in a blessed numbness that blocked out emotions. No. She couldn't think of that. She couldn't think of anything but doing whatever was necessary to get John back.

Her fingers bit into the hard plastic of the receiver. "Yes, Mr. Maitland," she said icily. "You have my complete cooperation. But first I want to speak to my son."

"I'll call you back later to let you know where I want the money delivered," he retorted, ignoring her request. "Oh, and I wouldn't call the police if I were you, Mrs. Rawlins. It wouldn't be good for your son's health."

"Don't hurt him!" she pleaded, but it was too late. He'd hung up.

She replaced the receiver with an unnatural carefulness and looked up to find the shock, terror and denial that raged within her reflected on the faces of everyone in the kitchen. Alex moved to take her into his arms, but the tenuous hold she had on her emotions was too fragile for sympathy. She stood stiffly within his arms and refused to feel, to hurt.

"Joe Maitland has John," she said in a flat, emotionless voice. "He wants the money we found in the mountains as a ransom." She didn't have to tell them what the consequences would be if they refused.

Alex tightened his arms around her, fury and guilt tearing him apart. This was his fault! When he'd hired her, he'd never even stopped to think of the possibility that he might be endangering her family. Nothing had seemed as important as finding the money and getting Harlan out of prison. Damn the money! And damn Maitland! If he hurt that boy, he wouldn't rest until he found him!

"Don't worry about the money, Jessica," he assured her huskily. "Maitland can have every damn penny of it if that's what it takes to get John back. Where did he want you to leave it?"

The relief that coursed through her didn't touch her tightly controlled calm. "He said he'd call back later with the details."

He nodded, his eyes searching her face worriedly. She was so self-contained, so calm. Too calm. He could handle her anger, even her tears, though God knows they stabbed him right in the heart, but this constraint left him helpless.

"We'll get him back," he promised her softly. "But we've got to work fast. We're going to have to figure out a way to catch Maitland after we get John back. We'll need the sheriff's help—"

Panic streaked through her at his words. "No! Jake can't know anything about this." Swallowing the fear that lodged in her throat, she said thickly, "Maitland said telling the police w-wouldn't be good for J-John's health."

"The bastard!" Charlie hissed. "If he harms a hair on that boy's head, he's going to have every man on this ranch after him."

Hating to disillusion them, Alex said quietly, "Maitland's a cold-blooded killer who's made a career out of eluding the police. The man doesn't have any scruples. Even if you do everything he says and deliver the money without notifying the police, he's not going to want witnesses."

So he might kill John no matter what she did. Impossibly, Jessica became even paler, her whole body tense with a silent scream of denial. She wouldn't stand helplessly by while that monster killed her son! She'd never be able to live with herself.

Her blue eyes were filled with fury. "All right," she said reluctantly. "I'll talk to Jake."

When the sheriff arrived fifteen minutes later, the boys had slipped upstairs, the ranch hands were milling around the front porch waiting for news and Alex and Charlie were nervously pacing the kitchen. Jessica was sitting quietly at the table, desperately trying to ignore the funereal quiet that had settled over the house, when Mary Lou showed Jake Sheridan into the kitchen.

A big man, six-foot-five if he was an inch, Jake bore the unmistakable stamp of his Indian ancestry in his straight black hair, his eyes, and his chiseled face. He had a reputation for being slow—slow-moving, slow to smile, slow to accept strangers. Those who knew him well, however, knew that impression was deceptive. He could move like lightning when necessary, and those black eyes could see right through to a person's soul.

He took one look at Jessica who sat at the table with her hands folded in front of her, her face pale and expressionless, and swore softly under his breath. She'd had that same look when he'd brought her out of the mountains ten years before with her husband's body strapped to a pack horse. "Jessica, what are you doing here?" he demanded sharply. "I thought you were still in the mountains. What's wrong? I got a message to get out here as soon as possible."

The only sign of her distress was her white knuckles as her fingers bit into her palms. "John's been kidnapped."

Spitting out an angry curse, he crossed to the table in a single stride and jerked out a chair. "All right, tell me everything you know. When did this happen? Have you searched the ranch? Maybe—"

"No," she said with a quiet calmness that was chilling. "There's no mistake. I just got a call from the kidnapper. He's going to call back later with more details."

"Well, who is it, damn it? Who would want to kidnap John?"

"Joseph Maitland," Alex retorted. Quickly introducing himself, he gave the sheriff a quick, concise report on the events that had led up to John's kidnapping. "Maitland's convinced that that money is his and nobody's going to take it. He tried scaring us off with stray shots and bloodying Jessica's tent—"

Jake cut in. "Charlie told me about that. Believe it or not, there are still some fanatical Indians that won't tolerate any violation of their sacred ground. That rat was probably a warning from them rather than Maitland."

"You might be right," Alex agreed. "But I'm pretty sure it was Maitland shooting at us. He's already killed twice for that money."

"Make that three times," Jake said grimly. "Slim was definitely murdered. The autopsy report was waiting for me when I got back to my desk this afternoon. He was killed by a blow to the head about three hours before his body was thrown into that ravine."

"I knew it!" Charlie exclaimed. "Slim wasn't stupid enough to walk off a cliff. But damn it, I still can't figure out why Maitland would want to kill him."

"So he wouldn't have to split the money with him," Jake replied promptly.

Jessica blinked in confusion. "What are you saying? Slim didn't even know about the money."

Jake hesitated, then reluctantly admitted, "He knew about it, all right. When I got that autopsy report back, I followed a hunch and ran Slim's fingerprints through the computer. It seems your friend Maitland isn't the only one who's been lying low all these years waiting for a chance to get his hands on that money again. Slim's real name was Frank Graham."

"What!"

Jessica paled. "There must be a mistake. Slim wasn't a bank robber! He couldn't have been."

Jake shook his head. "There's no mistake, Jessie. Fingerprints don't lie."

"But he was a good man. The boys—" She stopped, horrified. "All these years the boys have been around a criminal and I didn't know it, didn't even suspect!"

"Nobody else did, either," Alex pointed out. "Whatever he did thirteen years ago, he wasn't vicious now. Maitland was the killer, Jess, not Slim."

And Maitland had John. They all knew that Maitland wouldn't care that he had no grudge against a nine-year-old boy. The child was a pawn Maitland would keep as long as he was useful. After that...

She shied away from the thought before it could form, and the numbness that enveloped her was growing with every passing second. Why couldn't she cry? she wondered dully. If she could just cry, maybe she could at least feel something besides this awful emptiness!

The phone shrilled sharply, drawing all their eyes like a magnet. Jessica's heart jerked painfully, and she looked wildly at Alex and Jake for guidance. But Jake had jumped up at the first ring and sent his chair skidding halfway across the kitchen in his haste to reach the phone in her office. From the kitchen doorway, he ordered, "Let it ring two more times, then pick it up. Go along with whatever he says."

Alex moved to her side, frustration twisting in his gut like a knife at the sight of her white face and shaking fingers. She rested her hand on the phone and waited for the second ring. If only there were something he could do! But he couldn't, not until Maitland made his move. Wanting to throw something, he watched her drag in a bracing breath and hold it as the phone rang again.

She picked it up quickly, but before she could say a word, Maitland said, "I'm only going to say this once, Mrs. Rawlins, so you'd better listen good. You and Trent leave the money at the fork in the eastern trail half a mile past the spring canyon tomorrow morning at ten. Then go to the camp you left up there and wait. After I check to make sure all the money's there, I'll send your boy to you there."

"When?"

"When I'm sure you didn't bring anyone with you," he growled. "Remember, no police and no weapons. I'll be watching you every step of the way, and if you try any funny business, the boy dies. You got that?"

"Y-yes."

"Good. Don't be late." And without another word, the line went dead.

"Well?" Alex demanded when she had hung up. "Where does he want you to leave the money?"

"In the mountains," she said stiffly. "A half mile past the spring canyon. Tomorrow at ten. He wants both of us to come. After we drop the money we're to go back to the camp and wait for John to come to us there."

There was something about the flat, expressionless way she relayed the information to him that twisted Alex's heart. She was going through hell and trying her damnedest not to feel anything. Did she think he couldn't tell? He knew her now, and he didn't doubt for a minute that there was a powder keg of hurt and fury within her waiting for a match to set if off. If she didn't find some type of release, she was going to break.

He couldn't let her go on this way. If she snapped tomorrow up in those mountains, she'd be no help to John or herself.

Watching her carefully, he said, "Then Maitland's going to be disappointed. You're not going. Jake and I will take the money in and rescue John."

"N-not go!" she stuttered, her gaze snapping up to his, the gray fog of numbness shrouding her stirred by a sudden flash of anger. "You can't actually expect me to sit at home while my son is in danger! He needs me—"

"He needs you alive," Alex cut in ruthlessly, "and so do the other two. That's why you're staying here where it's safe." Before she could do more than sputter in protest, he looked up to find Jake standing in the kitchen doorway with Mary Lou and the boys directly behind him. He could see by their frightened faces that they'd overheard him, and he couldn't explain now why he was being so rough on their mother. "Mary Lou, weren't you saying earlier you wanted the boys to help you pull weeds in the garden?"

If the older woman was surprised by the outright lie, she didn't show it. "That's right," she said promptly, hustling the boys around Jake and toward the back door. "Those weeds have been driving me crazy—"

"No!" Her blue eyes nearly black with fear, Jessica stepped into Mary Lou's path. "I...I don't want them out in the open." If Maitland somehow got his hands on the other two, she wouldn't be able to bear it!

"I won't let them out of my sight," the housekeeper said quietly. "We'll just be right outside the back door. If the wind so much as blows, I'll holler. Okay?"

When she hesitated, Alex stepped behind her and said in a low voice, "You're scaring the boys, sweetheart. They'll be safe with Mary Lou."

Her eyes flew to the boys' wide, confused eyes and pale faces. Oh, God, Alex was right! She couldn't lock them in the house, away from the big bad world. Forcing a shaky smile, she said, "All right, but be careful."

Matthew frowned, unconvinced by her smile. "Are you okay, Mom? You are going to get John back from that man, aren't you?"

"He'll be back in his bed tomorrow night," she said confidently, and prayed that it was true. "Now go on and help Mary Lou. I'm fine."

Always the most protective of the three, he reluctantly followed the others outside. Once she was sure he was out of earshot, she turned to face Alex again, her eyes grimly determined as they locked with his. "I'm going into those mountains tomorrow for my son."

"No, you're not." Turning to Jake, who still stood in the doorway watching them cautiously, he asked, "What's the best way to handle the drop? Maitland's not going to like it that Jessica disobeyed his orders, but that's too damn bad. If he wants the money as bad as I think he does, he'll take it and run, no questions asked. Can you slip into the mountains without him seeing you?"

Jake nodded, one wary eye still on Jessica. "Those mountains are my ancestral lands, remember? I'll slip in tonight and Maitland will never see me till it's too late."

Alex nodded. "Good. Then I'll leave at dawn—"

"Damn you, you're not leaving me behind!" Grabbing his arm, she whirled him back to face her, all the fury and pain she'd refused to let herself feel suddenly spewing forth like an exploding volcano. "He's my son. Mine! Do you hear me?" she demanded, stepping closer to hit him in the chest with her clenched fist. "And nobody's keeping me away from him!"

"Jessica, sweetheart—"

Her eyes blazed. "No, damn it! Who the hell died and left you men in charge of the world? You think you can waltz into a woman's life, turn it upside down and then breeze right out again." She struck out at him again, hurt and resentment tumbling unrestricted off her tongue. "You're all alike. You and Jake and Joe Maitland."

Pained by the comparison, Alex winced. "Really, sweetheart, I don't think I'm as bad as Maitland—"

"Yes, you are," she snapped. "You tell me I can't go back into the mountains again. Just like you've got some say-so in my life. And Maitland tells me if I don't come back up there he—" she swallowed, her voice suddenly thickening "—he's g-going to k-kill John." She blinked rapidly, widening her eyes to hold back the tears, but it was already too late. They were streaming down her face. "Oh, God, Alex," she wailed, reaching for him. "He's going to kill him. All because of that damn money! I hate him!"

What remained of her control shattered the minute his arms surrounded her and pulled her firmly against the warm, comforting wall of his chest. She cried as if her heart were breaking, in hard, racking sobs that tore Alex apart. He'd brought her to this, he thought furiously. He and Joe Maitland. Dear God, how she must hate them both!

His shirt was soaked, and her tears were finally giving way to an occasional sniffle when she dragged in a shuddering breath and whispered against his chest, "I can't stay here while you go after John. I'd go crazy with worry."

Ignoring Jake and Charlie, who wisely kept their mouths shut, he lifted her chin and felt his breath catch at the sight of her tear-drenched eyes. Murmuring her name, he leaned down to give her a sweet, searing kiss of such tenderness that it set the tears flowing again. His arms tightened around her, and for a long, timeless moment the world, the pain, receded, and it was just the two of them lost in each other's arms.

Somewhere in the back of his mind he heard Jake clear his throat, reminding him they weren't alone. Slowly, reluctantly, he lifted his mouth from hers, but he couldn't bring himself to release her. Holding her against him, he admitted, "I'd like nothing better than to keep you safe here tomorrow, but I know that's not possible. I only told you that to snap you out of the daze you've been in for the last hour." With a gentle sweep of his thumb he wiped away the tears that still clung to her cheeks. "Tomorrow you're going to have to be ready for anything, and I couldn't take a chance that all your hurt and anger would come spilling out when we confront Maitland. You're going to need a clear head."

"That's right," Jake said quietly. "Maitland's desperate, and when a man's desperate he's got nothing left to lose. He could do anything, so we're really going to have to be on our toes."

Jessica's heart stopped at his words. Jerking out of Alex's arms, she cried, "Jake, you can't go. If Maitland sees you—"

"He won't," he said flatly. Reaching into his pocket, he tossed his keys to Charlie. "Put my car in the barn, will you, Charlie? There's no use taking any chances. Maitland could be watching the ranch."

"If he's that close, he'd better not let me or the boys catch sight of him," Charlie warned, his eyes narrowed dangerously as he headed out the back door. "Shooting's too good for his kind."

"I've got to call in the FBI, too, Jessie," Jake said as the back door slammed on Charlie's retreating back.

"No!"

"It's just a precaution," he assured her. "They won't go into the mountains, but if something happens and Maitland gets away, they'll be waiting for him." He could see the protests forming on her lips and quickly forestalled them. "I promise you only the three of us will go in, and Maitland will never know I'm there. Trust me. I know those mountains, and this is the only way to handle this."

"Maitland knows the mountains, too," she reminded him. "He's spent the last thirteen years up there. How are you going to take him by surprise?"

"I don't know," he admitted, the expression on his face grim. "But I'll think of something. I've got to. If I don't, he'll never let you and Alex out of those mountains alive."

The waiting for dawn was interminable. The evening passed with agonizing slowness, stretching everyone's nerves to the breaking point. The boys hardly said a word at supper, and although Charlie tried to dredge up their laughter with one of his famous stories, they were all achingly aware of John's empty chair. The forced attempts at conversation dwindled into a silence that no one knew how to break. Mary Lou finally told them that if she'd known they were only going to push their food from one side of the plate to the other she wouldn't have wasted her time cooking it. She shooed them out of the kitchen and cried over the dishes when she thought no one could see.

Jake left soon after that, slipping out into the concealing darkness and heading for the mountains on silent feet. Suddenly the horror of what the next day could bring was much closer. Jessica tried to hold her fears at bay by helping the boys get ready for bed just as she did every night, but it didn't really work. Desperation rose in her throat, nearly choking her. She was totally helpless. She couldn't make time move any faster. She wanted to scream with frustration. When Alex suggested they both should go to bed early, since they had to leave at dawn, she escaped to her room knowing she'd never be able to sleep. So she paced instead. For hours.

Long after the house had grown quiet, she slipped down the darkened hall to the open door of the boys' bedroom. They lay sprawled across their beds in the reckless abandonment of sleep. Safe, she assured herself with a silent sigh. At least two of them were safe. She wouldn't be able to rest until all three of them were within touching distance.

Alex found her there, a dreamlike figure in a gauzy white nightgown of lace and softness. Her dark hair tumbled past her shoulders, and her enticing scent floated to him on the night air. Somehow he'd known he'd find her there, worrying. Resisting the need to hold her, he scolded her quietly, "You're supposed to be sleeping."

Gasping in surprise, she whirled, her hand fluttering to her throat, her eyes wide. He stood only inches
away, wearing nothing but jeans. "I—I can't," she
whispered brokenly. "I can't stop thinking."

He'd suspected she'd be worrying herself sick. That
was why he'd come looking for her. Giving in to the
need to touch her, he slipped his arm around her waist
and pulled her against him, urging her back down the
hall. "Sweetheart, you've got to get some rest," he
said gruffly. "Come on, I'll walk you to your room."

She hadn't realized she needed someone to lean on
until he was there, holding her close. No, she silently
corrected herself. She didn't need anyone. Just Alex.
Sliding her arm around his waist, she hugged him.
"Alex, tomorrow . . ."

"We'll discuss tomorrow when it comes." He released her and gently pushed her into her bedroom.

A single lamp burned by the white iron bed, casting soft, enticing shadows over the yellow-and-white
decor. The sheer white curtains at the windows just
barely held back the night. As she stood with her back
to the light, every sensuous curve of her was visible
through the nightgown she wore.

It took all Alex's strength of will not to follow her
and shut the door, shutting out the world. She was
more vulnerable than he'd ever seen her, and he
wouldn't, couldn't, take advantage of that. "Go to
bed," he said. "Even if you can't sleep, close your
eyes and rest."

He was leaving, and suddenly she knew she
couldn't be alone. Oh, God, not tonight. He would

be gone soon enough, but for now she needed him. She reached for him. "Don't go," she pleaded softly, drawing him into the room. "Stay with me."

"Jessica, sweetheart . . . You need your sleep. . . ."

"No," she argued, stepping closer and quietly shutting the door shut behind him. "I need you."

The simple admission destroyed every reason he could think of for going back to his own room. She was a woman that others needed, but he suspected it wasn't often that she let herself need anyone. Taking the single step that eliminated the distance between them, he captured her face in his hands. "I didn't come here for this," he murmured, staring into the midnight darkness of her eyes. "I just wanted to be sure you were all right."

Her smile was soft, faintly rueful. "That makes us even. I didn't plan to ask you to stay." Standing on tiptoe, she pressed a fleeting kiss to his mouth as her arms crept around his neck. "Make love with me," she whispered against his mouth. "I want you."

He could resist many things, but not that. His fingers slid from her face into her hair. With a muffled groan, he covered her mouth with his.

He wanted to wrap her in tenderness, to explore her with gentle kisses and build her passion slowly until she forgot everything but the taste and feel of him loving her. But she didn't give him time for tenderness, slowness. The instant his lips touched hers she was hungry for all of him. Her mouth crushed his. The quick darting of her tongue stole his breath, and her supple body suddenly moved against his in a dance as old as time, destroying thought. She took a step backward, then another, dragging him with her, never releasing his mouth, driving him crazy with the advance and retreat of her breasts and hips against him. He wanted to drag her close against his heat and keep her there, but just when he thought he had the strength to hold her, to take charge of the loving, she dragged her mouth free of his and nibbled at his ear. Passion shuddered through him. He couldn't hold her, couldn't stop her, didn't want to stop her.

The bed stopped their slow, halting progress across the room. Jessica bumped into the mattress and made no attempt to catch herself. She pulled him with her, her breath leaving her lungs in a gasp as he bounced down beside her on the bed. In the next instant she was leaning over him, taking his mouth again as her hands rushed over him.

This was madness, sweet madness. The desperation that had eaten at her all day tightened into desperate need, blocking out thought, sanity, the world. That was what she wanted. *He* was what she needed. There was no right or wrong, no yesterday or tomorrow, only tonight and this man she could make tremble with just a touch. And she wanted to touch all of him, feel all of him against her.

Pulling off her nightgown, she tossed it to the floor and turned to find his hot eyes scorching her with just a look. He called her name hoarsely, but she just smiled and leaned over to give him a lingering kiss full of promise before moving away again.

Her fingers moved to the snap of his jeans, lazily working it free, the silken strands of her hair brushing against him in a tantalizing caress as she leaned over him, slowly dragging his clothes from him. He was dying, Alex thought as she pressed a kiss to his stomach, his hip, his thigh, dragging a ragged groan from him. "Jessica..."

She could hear the desperation in his voice, feel the echo of it in her own raging blood. "Not yet," she said, slowly moving farther down his body, exploring his hair-roughened legs, his feet, before sliding up again to let her lips and tongue linger at the hard muscles of his thighs.

Something inside him snapped as she moved closer to the heat of his desire. "Enough," he moaned, dragging her up into his arms. "You're driving me crazy!"

His mouth ravaged her. His tongue plundered, and his fingers were as urgent as hers as they swept over her back, the curve of her hip, the backs of her thighs, anywhere he could reach. Any thoughts of taking her slowly had long since passed. The flames that burned in him moved from his skin to hers and back again. There was no time for gentleness, no time to enjoy the pleasure she brought him, no time for anything but this soul-destroying need that was so much stronger than mere passion, so much sweeter than desire.

Rolling her under him, he plunged into her, her cry of pleasure captured by his mouth. His mind clouded, control shattered. Sensations rushed to engulf them both, pushing them higher, where the heat was hot-

ter, the air thinner, headier. Suddenly they were at the
edge. For a wild, breathless moment they hung there,
suspended in anticipation, before Alex sent them both
hurtling over the edge into the darkness.

Chapter 12

Dawn was still an hour away when Jessica awoke. The sleep that clung to her mind lifted like a fog, and awareness arrived in bits and pieces. Outside, a mockingbird sang happily. She was naked. And so was the man pressed up against her back, his arm draped over her waist, anchoring her to him, his face buried in her hair. Alex.

She sighed, snuggling closer, the sweet, aching memories of the night warming her before she was even fully awake. Then she opened her eyes and saw the clothes she'd laid out last night to wear into the mountains. Her blood turned cold, and the dream-like cocoon that had enveloped her vanished in the blink of an eye.

Before the day was through, she might lose her son or Alex or both.

Panic began to sicken her before she clamped a firm lid on it. No, she told herself furiously. She wouldn't let fear and anger overwhelm her today as they had yesterday. Joe Maitland was the type of man who would crush a weaker, more emotional adversary, and she'd be damned if she'd give him that advantage. She was going to be as cold as ice when she confronted him, and when she came down out of those mountains she was going to have her son with her. Nothing else was acceptable.

But she could still lose Alex.

As she stared blindly at the darkness that was gradually lightening beyond the sheer curtains at the windows, her fingers curled into her palms to keep from pulling the arm draped over her waist closer. There was no denying that she loved him more than she had ever thought possible. If she hadn't given in to her need for him last night, she might have been able to convince herself that her response to his loving in the mountains had been only a result of their surroundings and the nightmare that had destroyed her defenses. But when she'd pulled him into her bed last night, there had been no wild setting to draw them closer, no nightmare to cloud her thinking. She'd lost herself in him so completely that it was a wonder he hadn't guessed that she loved him with all her heart.

And now she was going to have to learn to live without him.

It wasn't the first time she'd lost love, but dear God, it was the most agonizing. The pain of it was already pulling at her, an empty, aching hurt that made her very soul cry. If Derrick's death had taught her anything it was not to look too far into the long, lonely years that stretched out before her. A single day was made up of thousands of minutes, and if she could just get through the little things—getting dressed in the morning, eating when she had no appetite, the hours between midnight and dawn—the years would take care of themselves.

But first she had to get through today, and the only way she could do that without falling apart was to face whatever happened alone. Alex was leaving; he wasn't hers to lean on. The sooner she remembered that, the better, she told herself as she quietly slipped from his arms and headed for the shower.

The bright, cheerful song of a mockingbird came from right outside the window. Jessica returned to the bedroom minutes later, and Alex woke with a start, instantly alert to Jessica's presence as she sat on the edge of the bed and pulled on her tennis shoes.

"It'll be dawn soon," she said quietly.

He heard the control in her voice and knew that the loving they'd shared the night before had already been carefully packed away in a distant corner of her mind. The day, with whatever pain it would bring, had begun.

Anger, frustration and the need to protect her warred within him. He knew as surely as if he could read her mind that she was already taking the world on her shoulders, preparing to deal with whatever fate handed her. And she'd do it alone, damn it! It infuriated him! Did she always have to be so independent, so self-reliant? Couldn't she see that she didn't have to tough it out alone? He was there for her, he always would be.

He opened his mouth to tell her, only to shut it with a snap. She'd made it abundantly clear that she had enough men in her life, and it would take a bulldozer to get past the barriers she'd erected around herself. He couldn't talk to her of love now, of the future, not when her son's life was on the line and he was responsible! If something happened to that boy, she'd never forgive him. He'd never forgive himself.

After tying her shoelaces, Jessica stood abruptly and headed for the door. "If you want to take a shower, you'd better hurry. I'll meet you in the barn in about fifteen minutes." Without looking at him once, she slipped out into the hall and quietly shut the door behind her.

Alex scowled and threw back the sheet, glaring at the closed door as he tugged on his jeans. He was tempted to go after her, to make it clear to her once and for all that she wasn't keeping him at arm's length any more. But there wasn't time. They had to rescue John, and then he had to see about getting Harlan out of prison. After that she'd be his, he promised himself as he jerked open the door and headed for the guest room.

She was already saddling the horses when he joined her in the barn. The case of money she'd retrieved from the safe had been placed on a bale of hay nearby. She was pale but composed, her hair neatly pulled back in a ponytail that brushed her shoulders as she moved. Her fingers were sure and steady as she went about her work. But even in the dark shadows that engulfed them, Alex could see that her eyes were turbulent with the fear she was so desperately trying to hide.

He wanted to touch her, to comfort her, but he knew that was the last thing in the world she wanted from him now. "We're going to get through this, Jessica," he said gruffly. "Maitland's not the only one who's got a few tricks up his sleeve. Don't forget, Jake's up there somewhere, waiting for us."

She nodded, her fingers shaking for just an instant on the cinch before she quickly steadied them. Straightening her shoulders, she said, "I know. I just wish it was over with. I *hate* waiting."

He handed her one of the rifles he'd retrieved from the gun cabinet in her office. "Here. Roll this in a blanket and tie it to the back of your saddle. We're going to have to be ready for anything, so keep it close."

Her eyes flew to his. "Maitland said no guns."

"If he really expects us to face him unarmed, then he's crazy," Alex said flatly, and he made short work of concealing his rifle and tying it and the money to his own saddle.

They left the barn just as the sun peeked over the horizon, silently making their way toward the dark, sinister mountains. With no pack horses to slow them

down, they made good time, quickly crossing the
narrow expanse of desert that separated the ranch
headquarters from the rocky foothills of the Superstitions.

Before Jessica was ready, they were at the trail-
head. Her throat went dry at the sight of the familiar
rocky path, and her fingers automatically tightened
on the reins. Black memories flashed before her eyes
like specters, reminding her of all the misery the
mountains had brought her over the years, but she
knew there was no turning back now. With a soft
click of her tongue, she urged her mare forward.

Within minutes, the ranch and civilization were out
of sight and they were once again surrounded by the
sharp-edged ridges and peaks of the mountains. Jessica trusted her horse to stay on the path, and her gaze
never stopped it moving over the rough terrain,
studying the lay of the land for possible hiding places,
searching, always searching. But there was nothing to
see but a never-ending sea of boulders and an occasional saguaro cactus with its arms in the air like a
holdup victim.

Tension coiled in her like a rattlesnake preparing to
strike. Jake was out there somewhere. And Maitland. She could only hope that Jake discovered
Maitland's whereabouts before Maitland discovered
his.

Bringing his horse up behind hers, Alex silently
echoed her thoughts. His gaze was razor-sharp as they
passed the springs and then turned off the trail to en-
ter the narrow, steep-walled canyon where Jessica had

almost been crushed by a boulder. At the time they'd thought it had been nothing but a freak accident, but now he wasn't so sure. Could Maitland have been responsible for that?

Before he could decide, the sudden sharp crack of a rifle shot ripped through the silence of the canyon. "That's far enough!" Maitland yelled from somewhere above them, his voice echoing eerily through the canyon. "Stop right there!"

This wasn't where they were supposed to leave the money! Jessica thought wildly, pulling at the reins of her suddenly skittish horse. Her heart in her throat, she glanced frantically at Alex, who was already drawing up next to her. "Alex, what's he doing? This isn't where he told us to leave the money. Jake—"

"Shh," he cautioned in a low tone that wouldn't carry to Maitland. Alex lifted his eyes to the canyon walls. "Jake will find us. See if you can spot Maitland."

With the bitter taste of fear on her tongue, Jessica swept her eyes over the craggy cliffs. They were as barren as the desert, and from the way the old man's voice had bounced off the walls it was impossible to pinpoint his position. "I don't see anything," she said quietly.

"Dismount, Trent," Maitland ordered sharply. "Slowly! And don't try anything. I can shoot the lady right between the eyes before you can even move."

Beads of sweat broke out on Jessica's forehead as she watched Alex dismount. Dear God, was Maitland going to shoot him where he stood? Where the hell was Jake?

"All right," the old man continued. "Take the money and put it on the path in front of your horses and open it so I can see if it's all there."

"No!"

Jessica turned a sickly white. What was he doing? "Alex—"

"What do you mean, no?" Maitland roared. "You ain't got any choice in the matter, Trent. I'm holding a gun on your woman!"

Alex paled. He was taking a desperate gamble, but if he didn't they'd both be dead before Jake could figure out where that shot had come from. He had to buy some time. "You're not getting a look at this money till we see that the boy's safe."

"Then I'll kill you both," he said coldly.

"Go ahead," Alex challenged him. "But if there's not any money in that case, you'll never have a chance to find out where it is."

Maitland's laugh was wicked, sinister. "You think I'm an idiot, Trent? The lady wouldn't take a chance with her son's life. The money's in the case."

"I guess that's a chance you'll just have to take, then," Alex retorted. He smiled when a slow trickle of gravel slid down the canyon wall fifty feet away, telegraphing the old man's hiding place. "You're not seeing the money without proving the boy's alive."

"He's all right, damn it!"

"Prove it," Alex challenged.

"He's not here. I left him tied up in a cave."

Suddenly, from the other side of the canyon, Jake called out triumphantly, "He's okay, Alex. I got him!"

Maitland jumped up from the rock he'd been hiding behind, exposing himself, disbelief working over his face as he caught a quick glimpse of the sheriff slipping behind a rock directly across from him.

Something seemed to snap in him, and with a scream of rage he started firing wildly at where he'd last seen the sheriff. "Damn you, that's my money. I'll kill you all!"

Alex didn't wait to hear more. "Get behind the rocks!" he yelled at Jessica as he pulled their rifles out from under the blankets and dived under the low overhang that jutted out from the cliffs. In the next heartbeat, rifle fire peppered the canyon floor all around them, and the horses put their ears back and took off at a dead run.

"Alex!" Jessica cried. "The money!"

The silver case glistened in the sun as the horses disappeared through the boulders at the end of the canyon. Alex bit out a blistering oath and tossed her her rifle. "There's nothing we can do about it now. We'll have to go after them later and hope nobody finds them before we do."

Maitland sent another wild rain of bullets down at the rocks that protected them, then laughed insanely. "I got your buddy, Trent," he shrieked. "And I'm going to get you and the Rawlins bitch, too! You're going to die, man!"

"I'm all right," Jake shouted down to them. "He just winged me."

His face grim, Alex studied the rocky terrain visible from their hiding place. Twenty yards away there was a break in the canyon wall that appeared to be the tail end of a path. Probably the same one Maitland had used to reach the ridges that topped the canyon walls. Shooting Jessica a determined look, he said, "I'm going up there. You'll have to cover me."

For a minute, her heart seemed to stop. The second he left the rocky outcropping where they lay, he'd be unprotected. Maitland could pick him off like a rabbit if he wanted to. But if he stayed where he was, Maitland would finish Jake off. And then John.

Her fingers tightened on her rifle as she moved closer to the edge of the rocks. She wasn't going to lose another man she loved to the mountains. "On the count of three," she said hoarsely.

Alex grinned. If there had been time, he would have kissed her. He had to be content with giving her shoulder a quick squeeze before he positioned himself next to her, his rifle ready as he crouched to run. "Don't move from behind these rocks," he warned. "Ready? One. Two. *Three!*"

Her throat as dry as the desert, she fired off five rounds as he darted to a large boulder at the base of the trail. Maitland, realizing their ploy, snarled angrily and riddled the rock where Jessica hid with five rounds of his own. Gasping, she ducked back farther behind the rock, her heart jerking painfully as she reloaded her own rifle with fingers that weren't quite steady. As she counted Maitland's shots, waiting for the fifth, her eyes met Alex's across the twenty yards. When the fifth shot came, she was ready. Quickly moving to the edge of the rock again, she fired as Alex sprinted up the trail. Within seconds he was lost to view, swallowed up by the rocks and another burst of angry gunfire.

Pressed back against the canyon wall, she squeezed her eyes shut. Her breath ripped through her lungs as she tried to block out images of Alex dodging bullets on the side of the cliff. Panic crept through her veins like a cold fog, chilling her to the bone. What if he got up there where Maitland was and there was no place to hide? Jake was already wounded; he might not be able to help him.

When did you become a helpless female? a voice in her head sneered. It's not like you to cower behind the rocks. Go help him!

Her jaw set stubbornly, she quickly reloaded, casting an anxious eye at the cliffs when another volley of shots exploded above her. It wasn't directed at her, however, and she ran in a low crouch to the rock at the base of the trail. Breathless, she took only a moment to calm her hammering heart before she sprinted up the trail, dodging from rock to rock, unconsciously waiting for a bullet that never came.

When she reached the top of the cliff, she came to a skidding halt, horrified. Maitland was hiding behind a boulder directly in front of her, his back to her as he fended off Alex from one side and Jake from the other, across the canyon.

Jumping behind the nearest rock, Jessica steadied her rifle against the boulder and pointed it right at the old man. "Drop it! Now!"

He whirled, his eyes wild with hate as he realized he was trapped. *"No!"* he screamed, frantically searching for a way out. His gaze moved from the edge of the cliff to the steep ridge that rose to his right, then back to the path that extended beyond the boulder at his back. "Damn you, you're not taking me alive!"

He started up toward the ridge, but he'd hardly moved when Alex stepped out from his hiding place, cutting off that escape. His gun ready, he said harshly, "Give it up, Maitland. The game's over and you lost."

"You'll have to catch me first," the old man vowed bitterly, and before they could stop him he bolted for the path, skittering around the boulder that blocked it. In his desperation he didn't realize that he was moving too close to the edge of the cliff.

But Jessica saw it. Horror welling in her throat, she watched his foot settle on the loose gravel only inches away from the rim and start to slide. A scream choked her. "No!"

She wanted to run and catch him. No one deserved to die like that. But her feet wouldn't move, and it was already too late. There was nothing to grab for support but thin air, and with a last agonized cry, Joe Maitland plunged to the canyon floor far below.

For what seemed like an eternity, the silence in the canyon was deafening. Jessica couldn't seem to drag her stricken eyes from the broken body lying below her, and then Alex was standing before her, turning her against his chest. "Don't look," he said roughly. "It's over. He's dead."

Her fingers curled into the material of his shirt, clutching him. How could it be over when the old man's screams were still echoing in her head? "Hold me," she choked. "Just hold me for a minute."

"As long as you like," he said, tightening his arms around her. When he'd looked up and seen her confronting Maitland on that path, he'd turned to stone. If the old man had decided to shoot his way out of the trap rather than run, he'd have lost her. He crushed her to him desperately. In an instant, he could have lost her.

"You can't follow orders worth a damn," he muttered against her hair. "I told you not to leave those rocks."

"I couldn't stay there like a helpless female," she said into his chest. "If Maitland shot you like he did Jake..."

She trembled, and he felt a suspicious wetness on his shirt. Drawing her back just far enough to see her face, he winced at the silent tears sliding down her cheeks. "Not again," he groaned. He started to catch the glistening drops with his fingers, only to stop, a slow grin spreading across his face as he caught sight of Jake and John approaching from behind her. His eyes came back to hers. "If you cry like that in front of John, he's going to think something's wrong."

"John!" She whirled, the tears starting afresh at the sight of her son hurrying toward her. He was tired, dirty, pale, wonderful. With a glad cry, she ran to him and scooped him up, her fingers shaking as she wiped the dust from his cheeks. Then she touched his hair, his arms, assuring herself he really was all right. "Are you all right?" she demanded. "I was so worried! Did he hurt you?"

"Aw, Mom, I'm okay," he said, enduring her fussing with all the impatience of a nine-year-old before pulling back to ask, "Did you bring anything to eat? I'm hungry."

She laughed and reluctantly released him, knowing she couldn't smother him with her relief. "No, but you can stuff yourself when we get back to the house." Ruffling his hair, she saw Jake watching them. "Jake, how can I thank you?" Her eyes went to the blood-soaked handkerchief wrapped around his arm just above the elbow. "Your arm—"

"It's fine," he said. "He just nicked me. John helped me tie it up."

"How'd you get him away from Maitland?" Alex asked.

"I've been trailing Maitland since dawn, but he's left tracks all over the mountains and he wasn't easy to find. I knew he had to be close by if he was going to meet you at ten, so I concentrated on the area just on the other side of the canyon." His expression turned grim as he relived the search. "He was hiding out in a small cave, and I almost ran into him before I realized I'd found him. I had to wait until he left to meet you before I could go in and get John."

Jessica frowned. "But how did you know to come to the canyon? This wasn't the drop point."

"I'd just pulled John out of the cave when I heard the first shot." Disgust hardened his voice. "I should have known he'd change the rendezvous point to catch you off guard. The minute I heard that shot, I knew he had you trapped in the canyon. I wasn't sure I could get to you in time."

"I was beginning to wonder myself," Alex admitted gruffly, slipping an arm around Jessica's shoulders. "He was ready to kill us, and the only way I could think of to buy some time was to convince him that we weren't going to show him the money until we saw John. Thank God it worked."

Amusement flickered in the sheriff's black eyes as he glanced down at the canyon and then back to Alex. "Speaking of the money, where is it?"

Alex grinned ruefully. "It's still tied to one of the horses, and they could be halfway to Phoenix by now. We'd better find them before somebody else does."

Carried home on a wave of relief after they'd discovered the horses calmly grazing by the spring, they'd barely come down out of the mountains before they were met by an anxious crowd of police and FBI agents. They answered questions for what seemed like hours. John explained that he'd been at the creek when Maitland had come up behind him and grabbed him, then tied him up and kept him in the cave all night. The old man hadn't tried to hurt him but had kept rambling about how Jessica and Alex should have left his money alone after they'd shown him where it was. A man was entitled to kill to protect what was his, and from some of the things John had overheard, it was obvious the wild shots during the expedition had been Maitland's way of trying to scare them off.

When they finally made it to the house, they were surrounded and asked the same questions all over again. Only this time it was Charlie, the ranch hands, Mary Lou and the boys asking the questions. Everyone was hugging them and fussing over them and demanding to know everything.

Basking in contentment as the excitement died down, Jessica leaned against the kitchen door and watched her three boys laugh and giggle over the pizza Mary Lou had hastily thrown together in honor of John's homecoming. Although she knew it could be some time before they knew what effect the kidnapping would have on John, he seemed to be relatively unaffected by the experience. For that she was thankful. He was safe and sound again with his brothers, and that was all that mattered. Her eyes alight with love, she reminded herself she'd have to be careful not to hover over them too much in the days and weeks to come.

Alex suddenly appeared behind her in the hallway. After they'd answered everyone's questions he'd disappeared, and she saw now that he'd changed from the clothes he'd borrowed from one of the ranch hands into his own jeans and the black T-shirt he'd loaned her when they'd made that harrowing night climb over the escarpment. His eyes, when they met hers, were solemn. "It's time for me to leave."

Chapter 13

The barn was quiet, shadowed, the air musty with the scent of horses, hay and manure. Sweat trickled between Jessica's breasts, but she deliberately ignored it and continued cleaning out the stalls. It was hot, dirty work, the most unpleasant she could think of, and that was why she'd chosen it. Anything to block out thoughts of Alex.

He'd been gone a month now, thirty-one long days in which her heart and the press had refused to let her forget even a second of what had happened in the mountains. The mad rush of reporters who'd flocked to the ranch the minute the story had broken had wanted to know everything, right down to the last detail. They'd made her relive that time with him over and over again until she'd wanted to weep with pain.

She'd finally started refusing all interviews, but the phone was still ringing constantly. Every time she picked up a newspaper she found Alex's picture splashed across the front page, his eyes gazing up into hers. Just when things had started to die down and she'd begun to come to grips with the loneliness that was her constant companion, he had finally gotten Harlan Perkins released from prison and had made the national news in the process. There were already rumors that a Phoenix-based political machine was talking to him about running for the state legislature, and after seeing the charming way he handled reporters on TV, Jessica didn't doubt for a minute that he'd go far.

She told herself that it would take time to forget him, but as the days passed she realized she was only fooling herself. A month, six months, sixty years wouldn't be long enough to forget him. She'd known from the beginning that falling in love with him was a mistake—he wasn't a man looking for a commitment, especially with a woman who required group insurance for all her responsibilities. Now she had to suffer the consequences. A lifetime of loneliness. The only way to get through it was to throw herself into her work.

But nothing she did seemed to help. She'd tried cleaning the house, taking it apart room by room and giving it a scrubbing that would have left a hospital operating room germfree. Still, she hadn't been able to wipe away the memories of Alex at the kitchen table, sprawled on the living room rug with the boys, in her bed. She hadn't been able to eat or sleep for thinking of him, so she did little of either. Mary Lou had warned her she was headed straight for trouble if she didn't quit pushing herself so hard, but she couldn't stop. When everything else had failed, desperation had brought her to the barn.

Stopping to wipe her brow, she reached for the thermos of ice water she'd left on a bale of hay, only to freeze at the sight of the man standing in the shaft of sunlight spilling through the barn's open doorway. His face was in shadows, but her thudding heart recognized him in an instant. Alex.

He was dressed much as he had been the first time she'd seen him, in chinos and a safari shirt. His dark hair was swept back and just brushed his collar. His face was harder than she remembered. It seemed leaner and far more dangerous. The glint in his eyes alone was enough to turn her knees to hot butter.

What was he doing here? The question trembled on her tongue even as her heart urged her to run to him and feel his strong arms drag her close. But she couldn't, not until she knew why he'd come back. She stood motionless, afraid to hope, her eyes locked with his. "Alex."

He'd have had to be blind to miss her wariness. He frowned, suddenly unsure of how to proceed. The time away from her had been hell, but while he'd worked eighteen-hour days to clear Harlan he'd consoled himself with the thought that when it was all over he'd go back to Jessica and finally get things straight between them. But now he wasn't sure it was going to be quite that easy. Had she missed him as much as he had her? She'd said all along she didn't want another man in her life. What if she'd meant it?

Never taking his eyes off her, he stepped cautiously into the barn, silently vowing not to rush her. But God, he ached to hold her! "Mary Lou told me I'd find you in here," he said quietly. "How are you?"

She swallowed. "Fine. You?"

Wincing at the inane conversation, he replied, "Now that I've got Harlan out and the murder conviction overturned, I've got some time for myself. I missed you."

Her pulse skipped at the husky admission. She took an involuntary step toward him, then forced herself to stop, afraid to read more into his words than he meant. "The papers said his condition had worsened during the last two weeks. The prognosis isn't good, is it?"

"No," he said grimly. "He hasn't got much time left, but he said if he had only an hour to breathe free air, it would be enough." Reaching into his shirt pocket, he withdrew a check. He crossed the barn, stopping two feet from her. "When I hired you to take me into the mountains, I promised you five percent of what we found up there. That comes to one hundred and fifty thousand dollars." Without another word, he handed her the check.

He had to be kidding. Taking the folded slip of paper from him, she opened it and paled. Her eyes flew to his. "How—"

"There was a ten-percent reward on the money," he explained, smiling for the first time since he'd entered the barn. "That's your half. Comes to five percent of the total."

So that was why he'd come back. Jessica's heart sank. Blindly stuffing the check into the back pocket of her jeans, she turned away abruptly, her eyes stinging. Damn it, she would not cry! Straightening her shoulders, she said indifferently, "You didn't have to drive all the way out here for that. You could have mailed it."

Alex stared at her back and frowned. If he hadn't known her so well, he might have thought she wouldn't give a damn if he left without another word. But he knew her now, her pride, her stubbornness, her independence, her fear of letting down her guard, knew she wasn't nearly as tough as she pretended.

So he'd have to take the first step and pray he wasn't mistaken about the way she felt about him. Leaning against a nearby post, he crossed his arms over his chest and said casually, "I had to come anyway since I couldn't very well propose to you through the mail. Of course," he added, as she whirled to face him, "I hadn't planned on proposing in a barn, either, but sometimes you have to take what you can get. You're not going to insist I get down on my knees, are you?"

Stunned, Jessica could only stare at him, the blood pounding in her ears so she could hardly think. Was he serious?

When she didn't answer, his smile faltered. Good Lord, was she going to turn him down? "If you're looking for a polite way to say no," he said gruffly, "I'd rather you stop me right now before I make a bigger fool of myself and tell you how much I love you."

"No!" She saw him grow pale under his tan and snapped out of the daze his proposal had created. He loved her! How could he think, even for a second, that she didn't feel the same way about him? "I didn't mean 'No, I won't marry you,'" she whispered, gazing into his eyes and letting him see the full extent of her love. "I meant 'No, don't stop.'"

"Don't stop what?" he asked warily.

A tender smile flirted with her lips. "Don't stop talking. Don't stop loving me. I've loved you for so long and I didn't think you were ever coming back."

He didn't wait to hear more. Snatching her into his arms, he crushed her against him, his mouth devouring hers, needs that had been too long denied turning his blood hot and heavy. He kissed her as if he'd never let her go, showing her without words how much he'd missed her, how much he adored her.

When he finally let her up for air, they were both breathless. Resting his forehead against hers, he growled. "That better mean 'Yes, you're marrying me,' because that's the way I'm taking it."

She grinned. "Yes."

"Say it again," he said softly.

"I love you. Now. Always." Lifting her mouth to his, she kissed him once, twice, three times, repeating the words over and over.

He'd dreamed of hearing her say it, but his dreams hadn't even touched the reality of having her in his arms telling him of her love. Pulling her closer, he sighed. "Ah, sweetheart, if you knew how long I've waited to hear you say that. I've been driving myself crazy the last month worrying that you were still grieving for Derrick and were determined not to let me into your life just because I want to protect you. I know it drives you crazy," he said quickly when she started to speak. "But I can't change. You're the woman I love. I'll always watch over you and make life as easy as I can for you."

Her hand came up to cup his jaw. "A part of me will always love Derrick," she said softly. "But he was the love of my girlhood. You're the present, the future." A saucy smile played with her mouth. "And as for protecting me, I can take care of myself, you know. I'm not one of those helpless women who just can't seem to function without a man."

No, helpless was something she would never be. Grinning, he said, "Do you think I don't know that? You can take care of yourself and a ranchful of people with one hand tied behind your back. I just want to share the load with you. Because I love you, not because I think you can't do it alone." Tilting her chin up, he smiled into her eyes. "Think you can live with that?"

"I don't think I could live without it," she answered, suddenly realizing it was true. How could she have spent all this time struggling against something she needed so desperately? He didn't want to shield her from her responsibilities, only to share them. Suddenly remembering his law practice, she said, "Speaking of living, what are we going to do about that? Your law practice is in Phoenix—"

"And your life is here at the ranch," he said, reading her mind. "It's the boys' heritage, and they belong here. Phoenix is only thirty-five miles away. I'll commute." Pulling her closer, he said, "Now that we've got that settled, there's the little matter of our bet to clear up."

She drew back, mischief dancing in her eyes. "What bet?"

"You know very well what bet," he growled, pulling her close again. "The one where I bet you that you wouldn't complain when I treated you like a woman."

She grinned. "Oh, *that* bet. What about it?"

"If I remember correctly, the winner gets to name his own stakes."

"Are you claiming you won?"

"I think we both won, so we're both entitled to name our own stakes."

Nibbling her bottom lip, she considered his proposal, then finally nodded, her lips twitching. "Sounds reasonable to me. I'll take an hour with you in the hayloft."

Startled, Alex laughed in delight. "Lady, I like the way you think. When are you going to marry me?"

"In an hour," she answered impudently, pulling him toward the ladder that led to the hayloft.

* * * * *

Silhouette Intimate Moments

MORE THAN A MIRACLE
by Kathleen Eagle

It would indeed take more than a miracle to help Elizabeth Donnelly save her son, who had been kidnapped by his father, the despot ruling the lovely Caribbean island of De Colores. Only one man could help her—Sloan McQuade—and even his skills might not be enough. Elizabeth knew only that they had to try.

Sneaking onto De Colores was relatively easy, but then the real trouble began. Soldiers were everywhere, and death could lie around any corner. Even nature seemed to be against them, sending hurricane-force winds to whip the island and keep them from their goal.

But theirs was a mission of love—a mother's love for her son, and a man's love for the woman he had grown to think of as his own—and there are always miracles enough to protect those with love in their hearts.

More Than a Miracle will be available next month only from Silhouette Intimate Moments.

AVAILABLE NOW FROM *Silhouette Romance*

Legendary Lovers

by Debbie Macomber

ONCE UPON A TIME there were three enchanting tales of *Legendary Lovers* that brought together the magical realms of fantasy and contemporary love stories.

CINDY AND THE PRINCE is the tale of lovely Cindy Territo. In one night she'd convinced hardheaded executive Thorndike Prince that she could be his real-life Cinderella....

SOME KIND OF WONDERFUL tells the tale of beautiful socialite Judy Lovin. Can her love tame the enigmatic John McFarland who's stunned her senses and captured her heart?

In **ALMOST PARADISE** Sherry White longs to discuss the wonder of fairy tales with Jeff Roarke. Now if only her wacky stepmother would stay out of the way....

Don't miss out on these magical tales! Use the handy coupon below.

Silhouette Intimate Moments

COMING
NEXT MONTH

#241 THAT MCKENNA WOMAN
—Parris Afton Bonds

Marianna McKenna was used to the bright lights of Hollywood until a tragic misunderstanding made her a convicted felon, sentenced to work at the Mescalero Cattle Company. But there she met Tom Malcolm and found that even the darkest cloud has a silver lining.

#242 MORE THAN A MIRACLE—Kathleen Eagle

Elizabeth had lost her son, and only Sloan McQuade could help her get him back. Sloan was sure it would take more than a miracle to do the job. But then, it had taken just that for him to find the only woman he could ever love....

#243 SUMMER OF THE WOLF
—Patricia Gardner Evans

From the moment Christian saw Erin he was no longer the hard-bitten loner he had once been. He had fallen—and fallen hard. But his job was to protect Erin, and her safety had to come first—even if it meant hiding the strength of his love.

#244 BEYOND FOREVER—Barbara Faith

When Catherine Adair came to Egypt, it was her chance to fulfill all her goals as an archaeologist. But when she met David Pallister, everything changed. He was determined to see past her cool, professional exterior to the passion beneath—and for the first time in her life, she was willing to think of herself as a woman in love.

Silhouette Intimate Moments

Rx: One Dose of

DODD MEMORIAL HOSPITAL

In sickness and in health the employees of Dodd Memorial Hospital stick together, sharing triumphs and defeats, and sometimes their hearts as well. Revisit these special people this month in the newest book in Lucy Hamilton's Dodd Memorial Hospital Trilogy, *After Midnight*—IM #237, the time when romance begins.

Thea Stevens knew there was no room for a man in her life—she had a young daughter to care for and a demanding new job as the hospital's media coordinator. But then Luke Adams walked through the door, and everything changed. She had never met a man like him before—handsome enough to be the movie star he was, yet thoughtful, considerate and absolutely determined to get the one thing he wanted—Thea.

Finish the trilogy in July with *Heartbeats*—IM #245.

Silhouette Special Edition

In May, Silhouette SPECIAL EDITION shoots for the stars with six heavenly romances by a stellar cast of Silhouette favorites....

Nora Roberts
celebrates a golden anniversary—her 50th Silhouette novel—and launches a delightful new family series, THE O'HURLEYS! with *THE LAST HONEST WOMAN* (#451)

Linda Howard
weaves a delicious web of FBI deceit—and slightly embellished "home truths"—in *WHITE LIES** (#452)

Tracy Sinclair
whisks us to Rome, where the jet set is rocked by a cat burglar—and a woman is shocked by a thief of hearts—in *MORE PRECIOUS THAN JEWELS* (#453)

Curtiss Ann Matlock
plumbs the very depths of love as an errant husband attempts to mend his tattered marriage, in *WELLSPRING* (#454)

Jo Ann Algermissen
gives new meaning to "labor of love" and "Special Delivery" in her modern medical marvel *BLUE EMERALDS* (#455)

Emilie Richards
sets pulses racing as a traditional Southern widow tries to run from romance California-style, in *A CLASSIC ENCOUNTER* (#456)

Don't miss this dazzling constellation of romance stars in May—Only in Silhouette SPECIAL EDITION!

*previously advertised as *MIRRORS*

Silhouette Special Edition

NORA ROBERTS'S 50TH SILHOUETTE NOVEL

In May, SILHOUETTE SPECIAL EDITION celebrates Nora Roberts's "golden anniversary"—her 50th Silhouette novel!

The Last Honest Woman launches a three-book "family portrait" of entrancing triplet sisters. You'll fall in love with all THE O'HURLEYS!

> **The Last Honest Woman—May**
> Hardworking mother Abigail O'Hurley Rockwell finally meets a man she can trust...but she's forced to deceive him to protect her sons.
>
> **Dance to the Piper—July**
> Broadway hoofer Maddy O'Hurley easily lands a plum role, but it takes some fancy footwork to win the man of her dreams.
>
> **Skin Deep—September**
> Hollywood goddess Chantel O'Hurley remains deliberately icy...until she melts in the arms of the man she'd love to hate.

Look for THE O'HURLEYS! And join the excitement of Silhouette Special Edition!

SSE451-1